Invisible Touch

A Scandinavian Dark Advent novel
set in Greenland

~ Petra *Piitalaat* Jensen Book 3 ~

by Christoffer Petersen

Published by Aarluuk Press

ISBN: 978-87-93957-86-2

Original Cover Photo Emma Francis

www.christoffer-petersen.com

"Mar[atse] was dead: to begin with."

— *Charles Dickens, A Christmas Carol*

Introduction

~ This is not a Book ~

Invisible Touch is an advent calendar, admittedly, it is a dark advent calendar, with very little Christmas cheer. It is supposed to be read one day at a time, as if you are opening a window on a Christmas Calendar. You can read *Invisible Touch* in one go just as you can binge watch a season of Kiefer Sutherland's *24*. However, *24* runs in real-time (plus or minus the commercial break), whereas each chapter, or *window*, of *Invisible Touch* is a snapshot from the events of that day.

Invisible Touch is, however, a complete story told over twenty-four days, from December 1st to Christmas Eve on December 24th, the night Greenlanders and Scandinavians celebrate Christmas.

Scandinavian Julekalendere (plural) have been a part of the Scandinavian Christmas tradition and culture for decades, and the first Julekalender aired on Danish television in 1962. Greenland also has a tradition for Julekalender, and I saw one of the first Greenlandic-produced Christmas Calendars called *Ammartagaq* in 2010.

The classic format of the Scandinavian Christmas Calendar tells a story over twenty-four television episodes. The action occurs over the course of each day, and as the month progresses it looks increasingly unlikely that there will be a Christmas that year. This is a common theme in many Christmas stories and films with many variations.

True to the nature of a Christmas Calendar, *Invisible Touch* is episodic, with new events and discoveries that drive the investigation towards its dramatic climax. But unlike Christmas Calendars in Denmark and Greenland, the elves have been replaced, and it is up to the police, and Police Commissioner Petra Jensen, to save Christmas.

Invisible Touch is my second Julekalender set in Greenland, one year after the last, in the year 2043. It is not science fiction, and there is very little technology or technobabble to distract from the story. However, readers will benefit from reading *The Calendar Man* and *The Twelfth Night*, the first two books in my *Dark Advent* series, as many of the characters and themes continue in *Invisible Touch*. It's not strictly necessary to read the previous books in the series, but it will add more to the experience.

The main story in *Invisible Touch* is concluded at the end, however, I will admit that the scene is set for the fourth book in the series, *North Star Bay*, following on from the last chapter in *Invisible Touch*.

Remember, it's not a book. Try to limit yourself to one chapter a day.

Juullimi Pilluaritsi! Merry Christmas!

Chris
November 2020
Denmark

Invisible Touch

Marlunngorneq

Tuesday, 1st December 2043

Chapter 1

Fastidious. He wrote it down. He didn't like the *fussy* or *picky* connotations, but *meticulous* suited him just fine. He *was* fastidious, only some people didn't know it yet. Soon many people would know, would see just how fastidious he could be. He closed the dictionary – a real book – with a soft thump of yellowed pages; the dust that escaped smelled glorious, old, steeped in ancient air. Before his time.

He found the book in the charity shop, on the shelf at the back, past the racks of adult clothes and infant suits – the kind with the button flap between the legs. The shelves bowed under the weight, as if the residents of Nuuk had emptied their houses and apartments of books and magazines, in one massive clean-up, dumping them all here, stacking them in tall piles on the floor like so many *inussuk*, book cairns guiding the way to hidden treasures. It was where he found the old *Oxford English Dictionary*, the one with the teacher's name printed on the inside flap, discarded once they left the city.

He had found other books on that shelf, more discarded treasure. Holmstedt's *Magiske masker og figurer fra Grønland* was a favourite, well-thumbed. The book was older than he was, but even now, thirty-five years after its first publication, it had never been more important. Greenland was losing its way. He saw it every day. The further the country moved into the future, the more its people focused on globalisation and the monetisation of Greenland's natural resources, the further they moved away from their roots.

Roots.

And magic.

Holmstedt's book was as big as the dictionary was heavy. He realised he had a penchant for older, big, and heavy books. It brought a sense of alchemy to his one-bedroom apartment, a sense of urgency to his tiny kitchen, loftiness to his cramped sitting room. He was on the cusp of something, something great. He could feel it – he *had* felt it for the past year, as he planned his entrance, his opus, devised his calling card, poring through dusty books for words and pictures, feeling the tingle in his fingers as he pressed clean, filed nails onto foreign words. More tingling, both in his fingers and his loins, as he carved deep cuts with the smooth-handled wood gouger in the air above his sturdy desk – also old, retrieved and restored from an old carpenter's toolbox.

He put the gouger down, laid it flat beside the book, adjusting the position: blade out, base of the handle flush with the bottom right-hand corner of the book.

The breath that he drew was ragged, as if he sucked the dust motes, soft, woody splinters, and bone meal powder from the craft workshop all the way from the basement to his third-floor apartment. He closed his eyes, tracing the cloud of mote and meal, sparkling with frost, catching the light from the street shining the way up the exposed stairs, lifting and lilting over the packed snow lining the steps, past the first floor, past the teenagers smoking on the landing at the second, before bursting against his own door with a soft fungal thump.

It was the mask.

Unfinished.

Calling to him.

It should have been finished a month earlier, but his fastidiousness had forced him to carve, and then to carve again – a new piece of wood. It had to be driftwood, preferably not from a pallet, but from an old tree, black and salty, long-travelled from Canada, perhaps. Maybe further south. His ancestors took driftwood, fashioned sleek frames for fast craft – the *qajaq* of his forefathers – or sturdy keels for the women's boats, the *umiaq*. They used the wood that had drifted for most everything that could be fashioned for a purpose, even the shaman's purpose, as he searched for lost souls.

The mask.

The shaman wore a mask.

Not always, but when it suited him, and suited the purpose of his work.

"It suits my work," he said, adjusting the gouger one last time, before pushing back his chair and walking to the slim closet in the hall.

He kept a pair of one-piece cotton overalls – no button flap – inside a zipped suit bag, folded once in the middle over a wire hanger. He took it from the closet, together with the boot bag, also zipped, inside which he kept a pair of soft-soled sneakers.

The key for the basement was hidden beneath a loose length of wood in the floor in front of the door. He collected it on the way out of his apartment, locking the door behind him, stuffing that key into his shirt pocket while grasping the other in his palm. He hooked his finger in the loop of the boot bag, carried the suit bag over his shoulder, then paused.

He looked down at his feet, felt the grip of ice leach the heat from his sweaty socks, curious – again – that he had once again forgotten to put on his boots. Of course, he had shoes, his sneakers, inside the bag, and the thought of remembering one thing pushed out the memory of another. It wasn't the first time he had replaced *fastidious* with *forgetful*. But it was more than that. He was perhaps *too* fastidious, and, at the moment, when his nostrils twitched with the drill-burnt blend of bone and wood from the basement, he forgot the simple things like wearing shoes on a winter staircase. It wasn't important. And yet, if he was to be fastidious, then *everything* was important.

"I can't forget anything."

But then.

The mask.

He *could* forget some things, perhaps *all* things, at least until he finished the mask.

He peeled his socks from the smooth ice layered on the step. He hurried past the teenagers, ignoring the heckles, the reek – and it did *reek* – of smoke as he hurried through the cloud they blew in his face, ignoring the words they cast at his back.

"Halfwit."

He wasn't.

"Retard."

Same word – still not relevant. Hardly important.

"Motherfucker."

That stung, stalled him at the first floor. He had never… he could never…

The mask.

He would show them when he was finished. Yes. Maybe even one of *them*. He could start with a teenager, *once the mask was finished.*

He pushed on, ignoring the clutch of cold at the soles of his feet, the last jeers from the second-floor teens. He let the boot bag fall into a drift of snow outside the basement door. The cigarette smoke was gone now. Now his nostrils were full of bone meal, and that sharp, black, once-wet stink of wood. He slipped the key into the door, stooped to pick up the boot bag, and stepped inside.

He entered the alchemists' workshop.

This basement, one of four cut into the granite beneath the apartment block, had been donated to the sculptors, artists, and storytellers of Qinngorput, the eastern part of the city. Here they tinkered with the past, transfusing it into the present. An exhibition in a gallery here, a stall at the Christmas market there. And, at the back of the *shop*, where the alchemist thrust the past into the future, stood the 3D printer. He remembered the day they rescued it from the University, and the thrill he had experienced when they plugged it in – the soft but insistent glow and fade of the control panel, blue beneath a thin dust sheet.

He changed at the door, focused on the printer, not yet ready to approach his workstation, not ready to see the mask. There were gloves inside his sneakers. He slipped them on, folding the boot bag onto a shoe rack beside the door once he had his sneakers on his feet. He unzipped the suit bag, hanging it on the hook above the rack before pulling on his overalls. The toes and heels of his sneakers caught in the cuffs of his trouser legs, and he hopped beside the door, working his sneakers out of the cuffs, cursing the fact that he *always did this. Every time.*

The mask.

It was time.

One of the other residents, the old man from the Block 3, had shown him how to use the Swiss-made sweep gouge, thirteen millimetre, to carve the lines across the temple of the mask, around the eyes, forming the nose. Another man – they were all men – told him to take care with the binding around the neck beneath the knot of hair on top of the mask.

"It has to look real," he had said. "The binding makes it look real, lets people *see* what it is."

"It's a mask."

"*Aap*. A mask. But the binding…"

"And the carving," the other man had said.

"Bring the mask to life. Give it power."

It was the power that gave the men pause.

Few masks were ever found in the Arctic. Most were destroyed after use, preventing the power of the mask from leaking out of it, hurting others, or even drawing more power – too much – from the shaman, weakening him.

Power.

He had recognised it, felt it when smearing the mask with soot, pressing it deep into the grain, the very pores of the wood, before carving. Cutting the eyes had startled him, as the bone dust from the old men's bone carvings had shone through from the other side, boring into his eyes, bringing the mask to life, and forcing him to put it down.

The old men were right.

There was power in the mask.

He had left it for a week, sitting on the table, letting the soot settle like skin.

When he returned, when he took up the gouger, he had found control, a sense of power *over* the mask. He was, after all, the maker of the mask. He should have control over it. The longer the lines he gouged, drawing the lighter wood out of the soot, the more power he imbued in the mask. He could feel it in his hands, the ache and cramp in his fingers, and also, weaker but insistent, in his crotch. The root of the shaman's power was in his loins, his sex, wasn't it? His sexual energy charged everything he touched, giving the mask the power to summon the spirits on his quest for lost souls, giving the *tupilaq* the power necessary to vanquish foes. Power – *his* power.

He sat down at the workstation, brushed bone dust from the mask's generous wood lips, then turned to look at the empty workstations along the wall behind him. The hobby drills and tiny saws were silent. The stools, dusted with the shadow of old men's butt cheeks, hidden beneath wooden cubicles, the last carvings still clamped to metal arms, ringed with more dust and splinters of bone.

The old men were gone – suffocated, apparently.

Sad but convenient.

Only the mask remained.

"And me," he whispered. "I remain."

He looked over at the printer, then back to the mask.

"Not yet. You're not finished."

He took the gouger, pressed it to the soot skin above the mask's lips, felt the tingle, then released the charge as he worked. Charging, gouging, feeling the stickiness in his crotch as he carved, one hand gripping the mask, one hand gripping the gouger – Swiss-made, 13mm.

Focus now.

Concentrate.

Press through the tingle in your fingers.

Ignore the tingle in your loins.

Recapture the past, stun the present, shape the future.

The blue lights of the control panel glowed, faded, as he gouged, carved, and charged. He worked through the dark winter night, into the early hours of the dark winter morning, smearing more soot into the face, binding more sinew around the mask's hair beneath the knot, wondering which spirit he should summon first, only to chide himself for thinking too far ahead.

Another glance at the printer.

"Too soon," he said, his tongue thick, dry. "Not yet. Finish what I started."

The gouger slipped from his fingers before the

dawn of the next day. He dropped the mask, pillowing dust and sooty shavings to one side – tremors and aftershocks, in rings around his work.

He looked away from the mask, pushing back his stool as he pinched the crotch of his suit, and the zip of his jeans, lifting his trousers, wrinkling his nose at his pungent stickiness, then smiling as he looked at the mask, nodding at the lines, tracing them with the tip of his gloved finger.

"Soon," he said, with another glance at the printer. "Very soon."

He left the basement, flicking the lights off as soon as he bagged his sneakers and his overalls. He kept his gloves on his hands until he was back inside his apartment. He showered, set an alarm for work, then took Holmstedt's book to bed, tracing the images of scored wood with his fingertips, admiring the artist's dedication and eye for detail – his *fastidiousness* – and then, closing the page on his thumb, he lay back on his bed, cheeks twitching as he traced the contours of the mask into sleep.

Pingasunngorneq

Wednesday, 2nd December 2043

Chapter 2

The neighbours in the apartment above woke early. Police Commissioner Petra Jensen opened her eyes, tracing the footsteps of the child – a young girl, if she remembered right – from one side of the room to the other. She checked her phone, then sighed, adding a little more self-pity than normal for a Wednesday morning, before throwing back the duvet and sliding out of bed. She straightened her panties as she padded into the bathroom. A glance in the mirror confirmed that the grey twist in her hair was still there. She tucked it behind her ear, thinking about the other grey hairs twisted into the ponytail at the back of her head.

Ponytail.

According to the whispers around the police station, Petra's ponytail wasn't quite what her staff expected from their commissioner. Was she trying to recapture her youth?

Am I?

Or was she just letting herself go?

It was the latest rumour, that Petra Jensen no longer cared for the job, that she was getting ready to retire – that she should have retired already – that she was no longer cut-out for police work, still grieving, she should take her pension before she started making more mistakes.

Like the last one.

Petra finished in the bathroom and walked into the kitchen. She filled the coffeemaker with water, cursing as she dropped the old, damp filter on the ground, missing the bin. Thoughts of her *mistakes* usually manifested themselves in that way of late, something she had learned to live with, to expect, and even to miss when they didn't occur. But at least when she thought of Natuk Petersen, the accidents and mishaps were consistent. She pressed her finger on the start button, holding it there, lightly, as she thought of Natuk, wondering if she was awake yet, prowling in her cell, or worse, sitting at the end of her bed, bolt upright, as she had done the last two times Petra visited her. If anything, visiting Aron Ulloriaq had been easier, talking him through the trauma of being shot – by Natuk – before he left for Denmark.

He talked.

Natuk did not.

"And in the meantime," Petra said, with another glance up at the ceiling, tracing the girl across the kitchen and into the lounge. "I drop the coffee, lose my keys, and…"

Piitalaat.

"And hear voices in my head." Petra tapped her fingers on the counter, wishing the coffee would percolate faster so she might get going *faster*. "I heard you, David," she said, grabbing a mug from the cupboard. "I just don't know what to say, today."

It had been over a year, *just*, since she buried Constable David Maratse. A year in which she should have healed, but, instead, she let him linger, refusing to remove him from her life. She still wore his dirty police jacket – threadbare in places and stiff with fish slime and spots of seal blood – albeit not in public, only on those nights when she missed him the most. Petra lifted her coffee to her lips, turning to look at the armchair in the corner of the living room area, closest to the patio door. He sat there often towards the end, head turned to watch the sea eagles drifting past the windows, or jerking awake each time his eyes closed on another page in an impossibly thick book. Petra never understood how he read them – massive tomes full of strange worlds and even stranger stories. They did, however, come in handy on the very worst nights when she missed him the most, lining his side of the bed with a constable's weight in books. His body – cancer-wracked – had been light towards the end, as if the print was thinning, the stories less dense. She checked the time, carried her coffee to the armchair, and curled into it, tugging the hem of her t-shirt over her *flat-but-fifty* belly.

The skies above Nuuk were still winter black, but the Christmas stars in the windows – *all* the windows – blinked between the wings of black ravens, chimney steam, and car exhausts. She reached over the side of the chair and clicked the switch to light her own star, wondering if the bulb had finally gone, nodding when she realised it had.

"I'll get another after work."

Piitalaat.

"What?"

Irritated now – why? Was it the year? The

anniversary of his death looming, or the fact that she had yet to move on from the other death, Ooqi Kleemann, Natuk's twin brother. Petra looked at her hand, looking past the bands of iron gall ink tattooed into the joins between her fingers, and, instead, feeling the tension on the trigger, seeing the look on Ooqi Kleemann's face as her bullet and the blast from Gaba Alatak's shotgun ended the young Greenlander's life.

Gaba has moved on.

"I know. And right now he and Atii are in Vegas."

You must move on, too, Piitalaat.

If only it was that simple.

Petra curled her fingers around the mug, feeling the trigger tension slip away with the heat of the coffee, if only for a moment, but enough to compose herself, plan her day and take the next first steps in a series of first steps, moving further and further from the past and into the future.

She looked up at a flash of light arcing across the fjord, tracing it back to the sweeping sodium light of a ship at the new port, financed by the Chinese to the chagrin of the Danes, and the consternation of the Americans.

Petra pressed her lips together, suppressing the smile that, of late, twitched upon her lips when she thought of the Americans, the US Coast Guard in *Kangerluarsunnguaq*, also known as *Kobbefjord*, to the south and east of Nuuk, and one American in particular.

It's okay, Piitalaat. I don't mind.

"You should mind."

But I don't. You know that.

Perhaps she did, or maybe she chose not to, but thoughts of Joshua Seabloom *did* make her smile. His dark hair, those grey eyes, and the soft American drawl when he talked. Since Maratse had started talking to her, Petra had noticed a subtle shift in his tone, less urgent, more encouraging, almost despairing.

"I need to move on."

Iiji.

"You want me to move on."

I do, followed by, *you know why.*

She did, and as much as she didn't want to ask, she still needed that final confirmation, one last simple, if infuriating grunt and accompanying nod from Maratse to say it was okay that she get on with her life, that at fifty-one she was too young not to fall in love, again, as many times as she wanted to.

Petra rested the mug on the arm of the chair, holding it gently as she turned to look at Maratse's books on the shelves.

You can take them to the charity shop.

"I can take them," she said. "Let other people enjoy them."

You can throw my jacket out...

"No." Petra pressed her hand to her chest, knotting the front of her t-shirt in her fist. "Too far, too soon. I'm not ready."

You're ready.

"Says you."

Iiji.

She left the discussion there as her phone rang, pulling her out of the armchair and back into the kitchen.

"We're not finished, David," she said, with another glance at Maratse's books.

Petra answered the phone, then walked to the window to look down at the snowy parking lot several floors below her apartment.

"Who did you say this was?"

"Constable Tiiu Mikkiki. I'm your new assistant. Inspector Danielsen sent me to pick you up this morning."

"My new assistant?" Petra frowned as a young woman leaned out of the police patrol car window and waved up at Petra.

"Yes. To replace Aron Ulloriaq." A pause from Tiiu, more frowns from Petra, and then, "It's been almost a year."

"Yes," Petra said. She pressed her palm to the window, felt the cool glass on her skin, and said, "I'll be down in five minutes."

Petra ended the call, took a last sip of coffee, and then padded back into the bathroom to get ready. Maratse's jacket hung on the coat rack in the hall next to Petra's bedroom. She could just see it reflected in the glass door of the cupboard, the image reflecting further into the bathroom mirror. Petra traced the outline of Maratse's jacket with her finger on the mirror, and then gently closed the bathroom door.

"Small steps," she said.

Constable Tiiu Mikkiki drove like she talked, with barely a breath between sentences or a flutter of brakes between streets. Petra tightened her seatbelt, curious that Inspector Aqqa Danielsen had chosen Tiiu to be her new assistant, and what other qualities Tiiu possessed besides the ability to chat at record speeds.

She found out a second later as Tiiu braked for a child who ran out into the road, oblivious to the police patrol car, and waving for the bus to stop. The patrol car slewed to a soft bump against the kerb as Tiiu avoided the boy.

"Close," she said, taking an extraordinarily long breath between words.

"Yes," Petra said.

"Do you think he…?"

"Saw us? No." Petra pointed at the clock on the dashboard. "My first appointment is in an hour. I'd like you to take me to *Asiarpak*."

"What's there?" Tiiu said as she pulled away from the kerb. She slowed as the boy climbed into the bus, as if anticipating a replay of the earlier near miss.

"The bus," Petra said, as they drove past it. "It's the school run. If you're going to be my assistant, then you need to meet Quaa."

"Quaa?"

"Next left, and then right."

Petra tapped the dashboard and pointed at a small girl; her face hidden inside a thick fur-ruffed parka.

"There she is. Quaa Mattikalaat. Nine years old."

Petra got out of the car as soon as Tiiu stopped. Quaa met her halfway, thumping her body against Petra's as Petra wrapped her arms around her. Then, with a nod to Tiiu behind the wheel, Petra opened the rear passenger door and buckled Quaa into her seat.

"This is Constable Mikkiki," Petra said, once she was seated in the passenger seat. "She's the new Aron."

"Oh," Quaa said.

Petra closed her eyes for a second, wishing she had left Aron out of the introduction, chiding herself for continuing with the comparisons, rather than letting Tiiu prove that she was skilled at more than just chatting and driving.

"Aron was shot," Quaa said.

"Thank you, Quaa," Petra said, as Tiiu turned around and headed back for the main road.

"He was trying to protect Petra."

Tiiu reached up to tilt the rear-view mirror, angling it into the back seat, just as Quaa pulled down the hood of her parka to reveal long, shiny black hair and inquisitive eyes. "Well, Quaa," she said. "I promise to protect Commissioner Jensen, if you think it's necessary."

"I do," Quaa said.

"And why's that?"

Petra thought about responding, cutting Quaa off with a question – something about school, or asking how her *anaana*, Iiluuna, was – anything to avoid what she imagined Quaa might say, something about Christmas and how…

"It's the most dangerous time of the year," Quaa said.

"How's that?"

"Haven't you heard of the Calendar Man?"

"Ah, yes," Tiiu said. "I've heard of him."

"Petra shot the Calendar Man, and then his sister came after her…"

"Quaa," Petra said. "Let's just get you to school."

But Quaa wasn't finished.

"And that's when Aron got shot, when they – Aron and Petra – were chasing Natuk across the rooftops."

"Natuk?" Tiiu said, twisting in her seat to look at Quaa.

"Yep," she said. "Natuk Petersen. I bet you've heard of her."

"*Aap*," Tiiu said, with a glance at Petra. "Many times."

"And here we are," Petra said, gesturing for Tiiu to park alongside the kerb. She got out of the passenger seat, helped Quaa onto the street, and then kissed her forehead before Quaa had chance to zip her parka up tight. Petra gave her a last hug, watched as she ran to catch up with two boys carrying oversized bookbags, and then got back in the patrol car.

"She's excitable," Petra said, buckling her seatbelt.

"But she's not wrong, is she?"

"No." Petra pinched a sleeve of ice from the ends of her hair. "Things happen at Christmas, Tiiu. We can't escape it, but we can hope that it's not as bad as last year."

Sisamanngorneq

Thursday, 3rd December 2043

Chapter 3

"So? What happened?"

Inspector Aqqa Danielsen stopped in the doorway, checking his watch before taking a closer look at his wife, then glancing at her hands smoothing circles around her generous belly.

"Kuuka," he said, shaking his head as if he might shake some fatigue from the evening shift from his body. "You're still up? Are you all right?"

"Am *I* all right? Baby, I'm fine. But what happened?"

Kuuka stepped forward to smooth her palm against Danielsen's stubbly cheek. She took his jacket as he peeled it off, then his hand, leading him into the kitchen.

"You baked," he said, drawing the soft, candied smell of cookies into his lungs.

"I did. Now sit." Kuuka pulled out a chair. "You talk. I'll make coffee."

The kitchen was the smallest room of the apartment, at the end of the hall, opposite the bathroom. The lounge and bedroom took up the space in-between. The chair creaked as Danielsen leaned back in it, reminding him just how often Kuuka baked. Perhaps more now that she was pregnant, too wired to relax before the birth – a son. When the doctor asked, then he just *had* to know.

So, with more baking, more cookies, and more people, the Danielsen's tiny apartment in the centre of Nuuk was insufficient.

Either I have to diet or…

It clicked then, as Kuuka brought a mug of coffee to the table, telling Danielsen to *hold that thought* as she made a cup of camomile tea.

"It's supposed to help me sleep, but you try sleeping with a lion in your belly."

"He's been kicking?"

"Kicking?" Kuuka laughed, then clasped her belly as if covering the baby's ears, not wanting him to start again. "More like running through the jungle."

Danielsen wondered at the jungle imagery, then turned his head, catching the faint melody drifting out of the lounge. He recognised the music accompanying the closing credits of Disney's *The Lion King*, Kuuka's favourite movie for as long as he had known her.

"So?" Kuuka prompted, tracing her fingers up and down Danielsen's hand.

"She got her assistant yesterday."

"And?"

"And I don't know how it went. It was a quiet day. We didn't meet."

"But she knows it was you who suggested the new assistant?"

"*Aap*."

"And she must see that you're doing more and more now that Ebbe Carlsen …"

"He's still Deputy Commissioner."

"I know but Ebbe's been gone for nearly a year

now, Babe."

"He's sick. I think they'll move him to a hospice just outside Copenhagen."

"I know." Kuuka patted Danielsen's hand. "And I'm sorry, I truly am. But you've practically been doing his job for so long now. And Petra's," she added in a whisper.

"I'm not senior enough to get his job. It's not going to happen."

Kuuka reached for her tea and leaned back in her seat. She gave Danielsen *that* look, the one she usually gave before saying the things that made him uncomfortable.

"Don't," he said.

"You know it's the way."

"It's not *my* way."

"Talking to Pipaluk Uutaaq…"

"She's the First Minister. She might even be Prime Minister once the whole commonwealth thing gets approved."

"Commonwealth?"

Danielsen loosed his tie. Perhaps it was the heat from the oven, the long shift – all his shifts had been long of late– but he felt the need for coffee, a handful of cookies, something to keep his strength up at the end of a busy day.

"Babe?"

Danielsen brushed crumbs from his fingers. "I thought that's what they called it. A *commonwealth*, like the British have. The country is independent, but still has the same king." He sighed. "I don't know what the word is."

"It doesn't matter what the word is. And it

doesn't matter if Pipaluk is First Minister or Prime Minister or even President." Kuuka lifted one shoulder, her half-shrug, the kind she knew her husband liked. "She thinks about the future. She saw opportunities with the Chinese and the Dutch. She made things happen. Now we've got a Greenlandic police force. It's *us* now. *Our* police. She'll want someone Greenlandic to run it."

"To run it?"

"Well, you can start at Deputy, Babe, but you don't have to stay there."

"Petra is Greenlandic."

"Uh-huh? You think so?"

"Come on, Kuuka. Don't start this."

"Start what? She doesn't even speak our language."

"She doesn't have to."

"She might. If things go the way everyone says they will."

"What way?"

"Forwards, into the future, a *Greenlandic* future. We can teach our kids what we want to in school, languages that are important to our culture and our identity."

"Petra is Greenlandic. You know she is."

"Something else I know," Kuuka said, as she pushed back her chair. "Is you – you're too loyal. That's why you won't meet with Pipaluk. Even if she called."

"She called?"

"That's right." Kuuka stood up, then rested against the counter. "Earlier today, before your shift finished. She said she couldn't reach you at work."

"She said that?"

"Well, no, not her. Her new assistant. Iista Enoksen. You know her. She and I used to go to school together."

"You're using Iista to get me a meeting with the First Minister?"

"Hey, don't look at me like that. You look at me like that again, and you can spend the night with your uncle."

"Kuuka …"

"*Naamik!*" Kuuka turned her finger in the air. "You see this apartment? You know how small it is. We have a baby on the way, Aqqa."

"I've applied for a new apartment. But with everyone moving to the city…"

"It's no different than it ever was. There's *always* a shortage of housing in the city. It's the same in Ilulissat, or Maniitsoq, Sisimiut. Uummannaq might be the only place…"

"You want to go back to Uummannaq?" Danielsen felt a flush of heat charge up his neck. He wondered if Kuuka would notice.

"Never," she said, extinguishing the brief flood of hope that burned Danielsen's cheeks. "And neither should you. You did your time in Uummannaq."

"My time?" Danielsen snorted. "I grew up in Uummannaq. I like Uummannaq."

"But you're here now. In the city. There's so much opportunity here. But you have to reach out and take it. You can't act like you live in a village anymore. You have to use your network, make calls, have brunch with people."

"Brunch?"

"You know what I mean, and don't pretend that you don't."

Danielsen tried to rewind, wondering what might have happened if he had come home half an hour earlier, when he had the chance, before stopping to chat with Tavik Aipe, the duty officer – something about a couple of old men in the same apartment block who both died of suffocation. He could still hear the duty officer's words:

"Two old men, in two different apartments, suddenly couldn't breathe."

"Carbon monoxide, from a heater?"

"We're still waiting on the toxicology report from the hospital."

Danielsen clicked out of the conversation at work and back into the kitchen with a snap of his wife's fingers.

"See?" she said. "You're too tired to even have a conversation with me."

"It's late, Kuuka."

"How will you be when the baby comes?"

He *had* wondered about that. It was also true that he had taken up a lot of the slack in the limbo period between the deputy commissioner being away on a course before he was officially on sick leave. Everyone had worked extra. And then, Maratse's funeral, followed by the Calendar Man, followed by his sister.

"Natuk," he whispered, lips curling as he said her name.

"Who?"

"Nothing." Danielsen stood up to open the

window. “I just need some fresh air.”

“What you need is to return Iista’s call. She can get you a meeting with the First Minister. She has time on Monday.”

“I don’t know.”

“I do,” Kuuka said. She shivered in the draught from the window. “I’m taking my tea to bed. You can come in and rub my feet when you’re ready.”

“I’ll just sit a while.”

“I know.”

Kuuka held her tea out to the side as she kissed Danielsen’s cheek. She brushed at the flour she left behind, laughing about how it must have been on her nose. She trailed her hand down his arm, squeezing his fingers on her way out of the kitchen. He stopped her there, in the doorway, holding her fingers tight.

“What?” she said, tilting her head to one side.

Danielsen smiled as he looked at his wife, seeing the glow of her skin, feeling the heat of it through the tips of her fingers. Being pregnant suited Kuuka Danielsen, he mused. It gave her a light, something soft, but brilliant, shining into the kitchen, brushing the old cupboards and the tired dishwasher with a subtle loving sheen. He could live in that moment forever, live in that apartment forever – it already felt like they had… been there forever. But then she tugged once more at his fingers, and the light dulled, ever so slightly, but enough.

“What?”

He knew they couldn’t stay, knew that the apartment had always been small, and he said so, looking into her eyes as he said it.

"So," she said, gently, "you'll call Iista?"

"*Aap*."

"Tomorrow?"

"First thing. Before my shift."

Kuuka moved closer, kissing Danielsen on the lips, pressing her nose to his cheek. "*Qujanaq*," she whispered. She shivered, and he brushed the last of the flour from her jet-black hair, just a little sweaty around her forehead but cooling fast in the draught from the window.

"Go to bed," he said, kissing her nose.

"You'll do my feet?"

"When I come in. I promise."

Danielsen watched her go, took another breath of winter air from the window, and then closed it. He sat down at the kitchen table, sipping more coffee than he should, and eating more cookies than he needed. He looked under the table, suddenly aware that he hadn't even removed his boots. He took them off, wrinkling his nose as the sweat of his socks ruined the sweet smell of Kuuka's home baking.

Danielsen's phone rang and he pulled it from his pocket, sighing as he recognised the duty officer's number.

"*Aap?*" he said, pressing the phone to his ear.

"You wanted to know the results of the two old men?"

Danielsen couldn't remember saying that, only that they had talked about it on his way out of the door.

"What about them?"

"I told you they both suffocated."

"I remember."

"The toxicology report came back. They think they found something."

"Found what?"

"A chemical – it attacked their lungs. They're still waiting on tests."

Danielsen heard a shuffle of furniture in the background, as if the duty officer was moving away from his desk, going somewhere quiet. When he spoke again there was a dull echo, as if he was calling from inside an empty room. Danielsen heard him close the door.

"What's wrong?" Danielsen asked.

"The report says these men suffocated, and the time of death is the same day, for each man."

"They must have known each other. We'll have to interview the whole building."

"*Aap*, I know, but they died on a Sunday."

Danielsen frowned as the duty officer paused for the second time.

"Aqqa?"

"What?"

Danielsen rubbed his face – more tired than he could remember being for a long time.

"It's the date, the Sunday."

"What about it?"

"Sunday November 29 was the first Advent Sunday this Christmas."

"It's a coincidence," Danielsen said.

"What if it's not?"

"Who have you told?"

"About the poisoning? That's in the report.

Everyone can read that."

"*Naamik*, the other thing. Your theory."

"Just you."

"Okay." Danielsen reached for his coffee. "Let me look into it. Don't tell anyone else."

He ended the call and topped up his mug from the coffee pot. Danielsen checked his phone, thumbing the screen to see the date. It was late on the third day of December.

"This time last year," he said, keeping his voice low. "We had two bodies."

He thought of the two old men poisoned in their apartments – the same apartment block, and tried hard, *very* hard, to imagine that it was a tragic coincidence.

"They died in November," he said, taking another sip of coffee, conveniently pushing the first Sunday of Advent to one side. "It's not related."

Danielsen finished his coffee, then slipped another cookie into his mouth as he collected his boots from beneath the table. He grabbed a towel to wipe away the melted snow, then stopped by the lounge. The television app had returned to the start screen, with the still image of *The Lion King* filling the lounge with a soft red glow that complemented the Christmas star in the window. Danielsen listened to Kuuka's snores tumbling out of the bedroom, and then padded into the lounge. He flopped onto the sofa and pressed *play*, turning the sound down low so as not to disturb Kuuka, but just high enough to drown out his thoughts about a potential copycat killer on a Christmas killing spree.

Tallimanngorneq

Friday, 4th December 2043

Chapter 4

Natuk Petersen sat at the end of her bed, back straight, knees pressed together, palms flat on her thighs. Only her fingers moved, ever so slightly, tapping her knees. The cell door buzzed, and she waited to be told to stand, to slip her hands through the slot in the door for her wrists to be cuffed, before taking a step back to wait for the guards to open the door.

"Physical," the guard said. "You're going to the see the doctor."

Natuk acknowledged the man with a dip of her head. Her fringe fell in front of her eyes and she lifted both hands, brushing it to one side, adapting to the cuffs with little more than a soft sigh of resignation. She followed the guard along the polished floor, looking directly at the cameras positioned above each door, staring into the dark lenses, idly wondering who might be watching.

They were always watching. It would be strange if they didn't. But the game, as Natuk liked to think of it, was to see who would blink first.

The guards were always the first to blink, to flinch, or to step aside on the way through each door, stiff hands gesturing for her to walk ahead of them, stiff fingers prodding her shoulders, pushing her forward.

Natuk watched them, flicking her gaze from one guard to the next, to the camera lens, back to the guard. She kept her lips flat, biting back the smile that threatened to reveal just how much she enjoyed intimidating the guards with her silence, how her stubborn refusal to speak unnerved them.

It wasn't her way.

So long as she was moving forward, eating away the time, one day, one hour, each minute, closer and closer to the day of her release. She would give them nothing more than the bare minimum of cooperation. Whatever else they might want they would be forced to invent. The very thought of what the prison psychologist might write in her report gave her a sublime, albeit short-lived, thrill. Having been thrust into the limelight at the beginning of the year, she enjoyed the flip side, the confinement, leaving her to her thoughts, and *only* her thoughts. She had heard some other inmates protest, get stroppy, arguing with the guards one day, insulting them, only to calm down and try to cajole them the next.

Natuk didn't protest, and she sure as shit didn't cajole.

It wasn't worth it.

"Wait here," the guard said, as they reached the prison surgery.

Natuk sat on a plastic chair that was bolted to the floor. She lifted her wrists, waited for the guard to lock them into a chain hooked through a loop in front of the chair, and then lowered her hands to her lap.

The guard smelled of cheap aftershave and half-a-day sweat. Not unpleasant, but strong enough to prickle the hairs inside Natuk's nose. She watched him knock on the door to the doctor's office, then turned her head to read the different infomercials scrolling across the television screen bolted into the top corner of the waiting area. If it hadn't been for the content on the television reminding inmates of what they could and couldn't do in the surgery, how they were expected to behave – all that crap, then Natuk could have been in a regular waiting room outside the prison walls.

She closed her eyes and tried to pretend, drawing on her memories of doctor's and dentist's waiting rooms, the stacks of magazines – pages curling, and the muffled coughs, wheezes, a baby's cry, among the patients. She preferred the waiting rooms in the dental surgeries, when the dental assistants forgot to shut the door and the sound of the high-speed drill whizzed and burred into the patient's minds, scaring some, unsettling the rest.

"Natuk Petersen?"

She opened her eyes, studied the young doctor – just a few years older than she was, then nodded her head.

"Come with me."

Natuk lifted her hands, rattling the chain before the doctor had a chance to turn. He sighed and stepped back as the guard unlocked the chain securing Natuk to the loop in the floor.

"She can't have cuffs on for the examination," the doctor said.

The guard slipped the key back into his pocket. "You're new, aren't you?" he said.

"That's got nothing to do with it. I've had three patients already this morning, and not one of them wore cuffs for their physical."

"Inmates or prisoners, not patients," the guard said. "Besides." He jabbed a thick finger in Natuk's direction. "She's not your regular patient."

"You mean she's dangerous?"

Natuk followed the conversation with interest, flicking her eyes from one man to the next, curious to see where the conversation might lead, if there was anything useful to be gleaned from the exchange – the doctor's naivety for one – and how she might exploit it.

"It'll be cuffs on until the end of the examination," the guard said. He gestured for the doctor to lead the way into the examination room, before pressing the tips of stiff fingers into Natuk's shoulder, pushing her forward with a firm shove.

"What's your normal weight?" the doctor asked, waving to the bed for Natuk to sit down. He picked up a tablet and double tapped the screen in the field marked in kilogrammes.

Natuk wrinkled her nose, sorting the bite of disinfectant from the men's aftershave, and her own mild soap and sweat mix. It always seemed to be hot inside the prison, stifling her some nights.

"You don't know?" the doctor asked. He pointed at a scales. "Step on that."

Natuk slid off the bed, kicked off her plastic slippers, and stepped onto the scales. The doctor grunted a number forcing Natuk to look down at the display: forty-eight kilos. She felt the pinch of her brow as she wondered if she had lost weight from her muscles. She would start working out again, something she had put on hold after an unfortunate scuffle in the cafeteria in November.

"You're a little light," the doctor said. "Height?"

Natuk looked at him.

"Light and difficult," he said, then pointed at the wall. Natuk straightened her back as the doctor measured her height. "170 centimetres." He tapped Natuk's height and weight into the tablet. "Are you getting enough to eat?"

"She hardly eats," the guard said, as Natuk stepped away from the wall and sat on the end of the bed. "Hardly drinks, never speaks. She barely uses the toilet."

"Depression?"

Natuk looked away from the guard, back to the doctor, wondering if it was a question or an observation.

She wasn't depressed.

But if he really wanted to know, where would she begin?

Perhaps it was her childhood, growing up with a Dane, being groomed and schooled for rebellion, to be used as tools in a fight that was never really hers to begin with. If that wasn't enough, what about seeing her twin brother die? Live streaming his death as Police Commissioner Petra Jensen and her ex-cop friend Gaba, filled Ooqi with lead. How about that? Not enough to warrant a lack of appetite or to clarify signs of depression? How about stirring up trouble to incite a rebellion and derail Greenland's independence at the bidding of a deranged Danish ombudsman with a real chip on her shoulder, manipulating two adopted children in the process?

Will that do it?

"You don't speak? Why?"

Granted, it was unlikely that he could read Natuk's mind, but she assumed – no, she *expected* – he had read her file. Of course, she should have guessed that he hadn't when the guard had to remind him of the security protocols in place for Natuk Petersen, the woman who tried to bring the people of Nuuk, and Greenland to their knees.

The doctor turned to the guard, gesturing at Natuk with his tablet.

"She's special," the guard said, finally drawing a smile from Natuk's lips.

"How?"

"It's complicated."

"So is performing an examination when the patient chooses not to speak." The doctor reached for the office chair tucked under the desk on Natuk's right. "I could use a little help."

Natuk watched the doctor sit down, then shifted on the bed, settling as the guard started to speak.

"It started with her brother," he said. "Last Christmas. He scared the crap out of us by leaving bodies around the city."

"Bodies?"

"*Aap*, all kinds," the guard said. "He pinned advent calendars to them, leaving one window open like some kind of code."

"And?"

The guard hooked his thumbs into his utility

belt and looked at Natuk. "The Commissioner shot him." He held her gaze, earning him bonus points from Natuk as he told the truth, and then more when he didn't flinch. "Then, after Christmas, Natuk took over."

"How?"

The guard kept his focus on Natuk as he talked. "She used propaganda, created a martyr, and turned the young people of Greenland against the older generations." Natuk sucked at her teeth, keeping her eyes on the guard, as he said, "It almost worked, too. If she hadn't been caught."

"She was caught?"

Natuk swapped a look with the guard. She would have rolled her eyes if he hadn't beaten her to it.

"Obviously," the guard said.

"Right," the doctor said. "Of course." He used his heels to wheel the chair to a cabinet on the wall, then removed a plastic-wrapped needle and syringe, before getting a small phial of clear liquid from a tiny refrigerator inside the cabinet. "We can make this quick. Just give her a shot."

"Steady, doc," the guard said, as Natuk shifted on the bed. "We haven't managed to give her a shot of anything yet."

"No?" The doctor shrugged as he jabbed the needle through the foil lid of the phial and filled the syringe. "I might be new, but perhaps there is something I can teach you, after all."

Natuk swapped a glance with the guard as the doctor approached the bed. She caught the flicker of something in his eye, something she liked to think might have been fear. It was enough to give her an edge, a few seconds, as he reached for the radio on his belt to call for backup. The doctor approached the bed; the syringe gripped and poised in one hand as he reached out for Natuk with the other.

The guard called for help, while Natuk took matters into her own hands.

It was simple enough to bat the doctor's free hand out of the way with her fists, and a swift kick to his chest thrust him backwards into the desk, forcing him to drop the needle. She followed up with another kick to the doctor's genitals, then stepped back as he curled and groaned into the foetal position. She turned back to the guard, took a small step forward, lifting her chin, catching his eye.

"Natuk," he said. "This means solitary. You know that, right?"

Solitary.

What they didn't understand about solitary, was that it could be peaceful, a chance to puzzle out problems, to plan revenge, or perhaps just to imagine the consequences of plans already set in motion, out of sight, out of bounds, but too delicious not to relish the thought of them. A week in solitary would do. Two weeks would be heaven.

Natuk pulled back her foot, preparing the kick that could double her punishment.

The doctor rolled onto his knees, groaning as he stood up. He reached for the syringe, forcing Natuk to grant him a nugget of respect for not giving up – no matter how stupid.

"I want to know one thing," the doctor said,

gritting his teeth as he primed the syringe. “Why is she here? With everything you told me, why isn’t she in some maximum-security prison in Denmark?”

Natuk kept her eye on the syringe, turning slightly, squaring her feet in anticipation of the help the guard had requested. She wanted to be ready when they burst into the examination room.

“She has a patron,” the guard said.

“A what?”

“The police commissioner has a soft spot for her. She’s taken a personal interest in Natuk’s future.” The guard caught Natuk’s eye, raising his eyebrows as if to confirm what he said was true. Natuk nodded in return, then sighed as three guards approached wearing riot gear.

“Why on earth is the commissioner interested in her future?”

“Ah,” the guard said. “You’d have to ask the commissioner.”

Don’t worry, Natuk thought as she aimed a second kick at the doctor. *I will.*

Arfininngorneq

Saturday, 5th December 2043

Chapter 5

Quaa slipped her small hand inside Petra's, swinging her arm back and forth as they walked. She tugged Petra from one side of the pedestrian street to the other, skirting the cluster of drunks outside the supermarket, but twisting through the soft flurries of snowflakes to the woman stirring candied almonds in a steel drum over a charcoal fire. They bought two portions, pressing their noses into the paper bags, eyes widening as they filled their lungs with the scent of roasted sugar and nut. Christmas hits drifted out of the speakers above the different stores, and they swayed outside the windows, giggling like sisters as they plucked almonds, popping them into their mouths, licking the crumbs of sugar from their lips.

"When are we meeting *anaana*?" Quaa asked, for the fourth, or perhaps the fifth time.

"Soon," Petra said.

"That's what you said last time."

"I did?" White Christmas lights glittered in Petra's dark brown eyes as she feigned surprise, before pulling Quaa into a hug. "You know what she's doing, don't you?"

"Buying me a present?"

"No? Really?" More mock surprise. Petra folded the top of her bag of almonds and slipped it inside her jacket pocket. "I thought she was buying, erm… curtains."

"Curtains?"

"Pillows, for your bed." Petra took Quaa's hand, guiding her towards the middle of the street.

"I have three pillows already."

"Three?"

"And curtains."

"Maybe you need new ones. Maybe you drool when you sleep."

"Drool?" Quaa stopped, then tugged at Petra's hand. "That's disgusting."

"Which is why you need new pillows."

"I don't drool."

"And the curtains," Petra said, pausing to check the time on her phone. "Are to make sure people can't see you drool when you sleep. You know, to save them from the sight of all that drool."

"That's disgusting."

"Yep."

"I didn't know you could be so disgusting."

"I'm the police commissioner, Quaa. I can do many things."

"Like catching killers?"

Petra slowed as they approached the pizza restaurant tucked into the *Godthåb Bryghus*. "Yes," she said, as they climbed the steps to the door. "Sometimes."

She opened the door and waited for Quaa to walk in, following her to the table where Iiluuna Mattikalaat sat waiting for them. Petra tugged her fleece hat from her head as she slid into the booth beside Quaa. Iiluuna reached over the table to tease the static strands of Petra's hair clinging to her jacket collar.

"Thanks," Petra said.

"You need to look your best."

"What?"

Iiluuna dipped her head to the left, nodding towards a tall man squeezed onto a small chair at the table in the window. Petra felt a flush of colour in her face as she recognised Commander Joshua Seabloom of the US Coast Guard.

"Your assistant called," Iiluuna said.

"Who?"

"Constable Tiiu Mikkiki." Iiluuna checked her phone. "I wrote it down."

"Tiiu called?"

"*Aap*. She said Mr. Seabloom…" Iiluuna pronounced the name slowly, rolling her eyes at her daughter, Quaa, until they both started giggling.

"All right," Petra whispered, hushing them with soft slaps with gloved fingers. "What did Tiiu say, exactly?"

"She said…" Iiluuna prompted Quaa with a wave of her hand, as if conjuring magic.

"Mr. Seabloom," Quaa said, with another roll of her eyes.

Iiluuna sat back as the server arrived with a large pizza margherita. The plate filled the table. "She said Mr. Seabloom had just returned from America and wondered if you were free."

"I'm not," Petra said. "I'm with you. We're going to spend the day together."

"I know, but now we have pizza, and I had a chat with *Nissimaaq*…"

"Santa Claus," Quaa said.

"And maybe you should have some fun." Iiluuna paused as the server returned with their drinks. "It's okay, Petra," she said. "David wouldn't mind."

Quaa looked at her mother and then at Petra as both women fell quiet for a moment. She slipped her hand around Petra's fingers and squeezed. "You can always come back to our place afterwards," she said. "If you want to."

Petra smiled, then leaned over to kiss Quaa on the top of her head. "It's an ambush," she said. She took a long breath, then tucked her hat into her pocket. It struck her then that she wasn't wearing Maratse's old police jacket. *Maybe it's a sign,* she thought.

"Have fun with Mr. Seabloom," Iiluuna said, eyes twinkling in the light from the booth.

"I just might," Petra said. She ruffled Quaa's hair, then leaned over the table to kiss Iiluuna on the cheek. "Thank you," she whispered, as she pulled away.

Petra picked her way around the tables until she arrived at Seabloom's table in the window. He stood up to greet her, kissing her cheek and sending a little shiver through Petra's body. She recovered with an awkward *hello* and then sat down.

"I've been selfish," Seabloom said. "I just got in, and I wanted to see you before I drove back to the base. I hope it's okay."

"It's okay," Petra said, then, "It's nice. Thank you."

"Your assistant…"

"Constable Mikkiki." Petra couldn't remember giving Tiiu access to her calendar – they had barely been introduced. But it made sense that Danielsen would bring her up to speed as quickly as possible. Friday had been hectic, and she had been tied up with preparations for the budget meeting. So, she decided, she could easily have missed something. *Lots of things, as it turns out.* Petra asked for another minute when the server arrived, then took a few more seconds to compose herself. "How long were you in America?"

"Four weeks. Part of it was leave. I had to see my eldest daughter, she's just started high school."

"Your daughter?"

"Flick." Seabloom laughed as Petra wrinkled her brow. "Short for Felicity. She hates her given name, so we call her Flick." Seabloom took a sip of water from the glass in front of him. "She's fifteen. She has a sister, Marion, and a brother, Jack. There's one year between each. They all live with their mom. "

"And their mom?"

"Her name is Samantha. We were childhood sweethearts. Met in junior high. Married as soon as we could. The divorce…" Seabloom paused, drumming his fingers lightly on the table as he looked at Petra. "It seems to be taking a little longer." He shrugged like it was old news.

"I see," Petra said. She looked up as the server turned towards them, then glanced over her shoulder at Quaa and Iiluuna, and then said, "Shall we go across the street?"

"What's across the street?"

"A bar, and a restaurant." She smiled as she added, "Bigger chairs."

"Then let's go."

Seabloom smiled at the server, pointed at the tip he left on the table, and then followed Petra out of the door and into the street. Petra brushed at the snow in her hair before tugging her hat out of her pocket and smoothing it onto her head. Seabloom turned his collar up and then bent his arm into a crook. Petra slipped her hand through it.

"I thought you might say no," Seabloom said, as they crossed the street. "So," he said, before Petra could answer. "I took a chance, telling myself, *Joshua, it's just a drink, maybe a bite to eat. What could possibly go wrong?*"

"Plenty," Petra said, brushing more snow from her forehead. "You remember Natuk?"

"Of course. How could I forget?" Seabloom slowed as they reached the bar. "What happened to her?"

"She's in prison, here in Nuuk. I visited her a few times, but she never speaks." Petra kicked the snow from her boots before opening the door to the bar. "She's got talent," she said, raising her voice over the Saturday afternoon cheer. "I hate to see it wasted."

"She's a sociopath, if you ask me." Seabloom pointed at a group of four as they got ready to leave a table. They waited to one side, smiling as the group pulled on their jackets, hats, and gloves, swapping looks and frowns as the snow fell heavier, slapping thickly against the window. Petra sat down just as a young man arrived to clear the table.

"I don't think she's a sociopath," she said, as Seabloom draped his jacket over the back of the chair. "She's just driven."

"A dangerous driver?" He laughed. "Sorry, bad joke."

Petra brushed it aside with a flick of her fingers. "Let's not talk about Natuk."

"Agreed."

The young man returned for their order – two beers and a basket of fries. Seabloom was the first to talk, once the server had gone.

"Actually, I'd like to talk about you, Commissioner."

"*Commissioner*? Is this *shop talk*?"

"No, I was just being cute." He leaned back as the server returned, arching his eyebrows at the thick fries heaped in the basket. He raised his glass, knocking it against Petra's. "Cheers."

Petra took a sip, watching Seabloom over the lip of the glass, curious what he might say, and even more curious how ready she was for him to say it – whatever it might be. She felt a warm glow spread from her stomach, tingling through her fingers as she put the glass back down on the table. She reached out and took Seabloom's free hand, before she had even thought about it, just acting on impulse, trusting her gut, trusting that David would understand.

"What do you want to know?"

"Family, for starters." Seabloom lifted his finger from the glass and pointed at the pizza restaurant across the street. "Who were they, in the pizza place?"

"Quaa and her mother, Iiluuna. Friends of David's. At least Iiluuna was. He looked after her for a short while when she was a girl. She came to David's funeral, and, well…" Petra squeezed Seabloom's hand as she sighed. "To be honest, it all happened rather quickly. I guess we had a lot in common – we both grew up without our parents. Both went to the children's home, here in Nuuk. David brought us together, and we've kind of just stayed together." She smiled. "It probably seems strange to you, but I think it's a Greenlandic thing. Life is too short to think things through from every angle. You have to live for the moment." She shrugged again. "Some people would tell you it's because we live *on the edge*." She laughed. "It sounds so melodramatic, but I guess there's some truth in it. Life can be unpredictable up here. If something works, you just have to go with it."

"Yeah," Seabloom said. "I've noticed." He took a sip of beer, but kept his eyes focused on Petra.

"And?"

"What?"

"Is that what we're doing? Going with it?"

Seabloom put his glass on the table, smiled, and said, "Fries are getting cold."

"Wow," Petra said, laughing as she pulled her hand free of his fingers. "That's evasive."

"Hey, I didn't mean to offend."

"You didn't." She reached for the basket and plucked a large potato wedge from the side. "I'm hungry."

Seabloom reached for her hand and Petra let him take it. They swapped stories about his flight, her new assistant, the ice on the bridge across *Kangerluarsunnguaq* to the Coast Guard base, Petra's noisy neighbours, Seabloom's children, and, when Petra pressed, about Samantha. Seabloom quickly turned the topic back to his eldest daughter.

"It's like she's thirty already," he said, as Petra took the last of the fries. "I mean I *know* she's fifteen, but…" He shook his head, and said, "Damn. So grown up already."

"That's girls for you," Petra said. "We grow up fast."

Seabloom smiled, then finished his beer. "I think you'd like her. I think she'd like you."

"Yep." Petra laughed. "You've definitely been here too long already."

"Too long?"

"You picked up on the *seize the day* mentality."

"I have?"

"One beer and a basket of fries, and now you want me to meet your daughter."

"Commissioner," Seabloom said with a frown. "I'm probably tired, jet lagged – *definitely* jet lagged, but I'm going to need help when you're teasing me."

"Yep," Petra said, as her phone buzzed with a new message. She slipped her hand into her pocket, apologising as she swiped her screen.

Petra slumped in her chair, tugging her hand across the table as she held her phone in her lap. The thumbnail image of the file was enough to spread a chill through her body, as the heat from the room evaporated from her cheeks, pooling in a circle of cold around her chair.

“What is it?”

Petra swallowed before speaking. She bit her bottom lip, and then said, “It’s a video.” She looked up. “Someone sent me a video of David.”

Sapaat

Sunday, 6th December 2043

Chapter 6

He woke early, slipping out of bed, tugging the sheets, flattening them with sweeps of stiff palms, tightening the edges, before he went to the bathroom. He'd forgotten something. He turned around, padded back into the bedroom, saw his wrinkled pillow pinned in the corner between the wall and his bed. He pulled it free, plumped it, flattened it, straightened the pillowcase, then placed it at the top of the bed, in the middle, as best he could centre it. He shook his head on the way back into the bathroom. What else would he forget today?

Breakfast was little more than oats, long-life milk, and the promise of eggs he would bring back from the store. He flicked the stubborn oats caught between his teeth with his tongue as he drank thin powdered coffee. He did the dishes – *clearing the decks*, as he liked to call it, before opening the cupboard beneath the sink, moving the bottles of cleaning products to one side, bringing the larger, four litre bottle to the front. He turned it to one side, peered at the yellow triangle with the black skull and crossbones. He tried to fix his grin like the skull, but it made his jaw ache.

"Not yet," he said, closing the cupboard. "The mask."

It lay in the middle of the work desk, just where he had left it. He approached it from an angle, zipping the front of his overalls, tightening his gloves with a sharp tug of the hem at the base of his palms. The soles of his sneakers stuck to the floor – tacky when he lifted his heels. He sniffed, searching the floor as he did so, searching for a leak. Had someone been in the basement? Dropped a bottle of soda? Had he?

"No."

He hadn't been in the basement for five days.

He moved around the floor, lifting his feet, brushing bone meal powder, wood shavings, and sawdust to one side, tracing arcs with his toes until he found a stain, brown and flat like painted roots. He followed it to a plastic jerry can of oil, fat that one of the old men swore was better than varnish. There was a split in the side of the can. He pressed the tip of one gloved finger against it, pressed it in to release a glob of fat, grease, oil that dribbled across the floor. He must have knocked it somehow but couldn't remember when.

"Always forgetting something."

He walked back to the work desk, with but a glance and a smile at the printer in the corner, its blue display glowing, fading, waiting to be used.

"Today," he said. "In just a minute."

He stopped by the mask, slipped his hands behind his back and studied it, as if for the first time. The grooves were suitably erratic, the lips thick and pouty, eyes almost squared, and the square of wood that was the knot of hair… well, it was a perfect replica of the real thing. This *was* the real thing. A work of art with which he would continue his work.

"Today. Later."

Another look at the printer.

He picked up the mask and carried it to the printer. It was an older model, discarded by the University, but more than adequate for his needs. He removed the dust sheet, then lifted the lid of the box scanner. He placed the mask flat on the surface, replaced the lid, and pressed the button to scan.

"And away we go."

The scanner chittered as rays of blue light traced the contours of the mask. He turned to the display, peering into the screen as the mask appeared, one layer at a time, left to right. He pressed his fingers onto the screen, turning the image on an axis, nodding at the subtle and smooth curve of the back side of the mask. He fiddled with the settings, choosing a porous surface for the back, just enough to hold a coating of paint, and a glossy outer face. He adjusted the colours on the front, nodding as the layers revealed the light brown grooves cut into the sooty surface of the mask. He nodded again at the eyeholes and the hole for the mouth through which the wearer could breathe.

"Breathe."

He lifted his head to laugh, then turned back to the display, adding two holes either side of the eyes, to which he planned to attach a length of elastic.

Finally, as the digital reproduction was fully realised, he tapped his finger to the right of the screen as he thought about how many masks he should print.

He felt a familiar tingling in his loins as he considered it. Not an easy question, and yet, from the printer's point of view, it was perhaps the simplest setting.

How many masks?

Of course, he didn't have to use them all, but it would be a shame not to. They would see the first mask as a one-off, but the second would make them wonder.

"And so they should."

It was required.

If they didn't wonder, if they didn't question, then there was no point making any masks. None at all.

The tingling in his loins became an ache, something unpleasant, drawing his lips into a sneer. He stabbed the display, thumping the glass until he reached double figures. Eleven masks. Twelve. Twelve days of Christmas.

It came to him then.

Nine.

The age when he…

"No. I won't talk about it." He took a breath. "I'll do it, but I won't talk about it. Okay?"

He stabbed the display, lowering the number of copies, confirming the print run of nine plastic masks.

He left the printer to run in the basement, bagging his sneakers and overalls, smiling as he slipped his feet into the boots he had remembered to bring with him, and then locking the door. He climbed the stairs to his apartment, left the sneakers and overalls just inside the door, and then grabbed the four-litre plastic can with the skull and crossbones from under the sink. He set it on the kitchen table, stared at it for a few minutes, then walked into the hall and opened the closet. He reached up to the top shelf, standing on tiptoe and pressing his arm as far as he could reach until his fingers bumped against a small tin. He pulled it out, returned to the kitchen, turning the tin in his hand as he read the label.

"Boat paint, for all surfaces."

He found an empty plastic container in the cupboard over the sink, prised the lid off the blue paint and poured a gloop of it into the container. Once he had a finger's depth of paint, he swapped the tin for the plastic container, pausing again to read the label, quietly this time, as he imagined an alchemist might on the eve of some great but terrible discovery. He unscrewed the plastic cap, poured a little into the container, then swore, sloshing some of the contents onto the table as he opened the window, then grabbed the filter mask he had bought at the hardware store, the same day he bought the paint.

Same day. Different store.

At least he thought so. It was important. But he was always forgetting something. But right now, on the kitchen table – *that* was important. He could forget the rest. Worry about it later. He pulled the mask over his face, grabbed a wooden spoon from the utensil draw and stirred.

The snow settled through the day, with but a whisper of light flurries in the air as he walked along the side of the road to the Christmas market. The paint had been easy to apply, but it took longer to dry than he had expected. He checked the time on his phone. The market would close in nine minutes.

Nine.

The same number of masks he had printed.

"But only one today. A trial run."

He slowed as he approached the sports hall on *H.J. Rinkip Aqqutaa*. Cigarette smoke hung in small clouds above groups of smokers outside the door. He held his breath as he weaved his way through them, head down, the hood of his parka zipped all the way to the end. One would have to stand very close to see more than his eyes. He slipped inside the hall, paused to study the layout, noting the positions of the stalls, and, more importantly, the restrooms. He followed the signs to the changing rooms, knowing that they were open to the market guests.

The smell of narwhal soup, spiced with curry, drifted into his hood, making his mouth water. He swallowed, ignored the rumble in his belly, and focused on the tremble in his fingers, the tingle in his loins, and then the two boys that blistered into the changing rooms, plastic bags flapping at their sides bulging with candy. He followed discreetly, watched them enter the cubicles, then slid the mask onto the counter between the two washbasins. If he had thought about it, he would have brought two masks.

"I should have," he whispered.

But then the boys were finished, and he slipped out of the bathroom, stuffing the plastic bag into the pocket of his parka, as he retreated to the other side of the sports hall.

One of the boys was taller than the other, and he wondered if he was the dominant one. Would it be him that put on the mask? Would either of them? Or would they ignore it, just like so many Greenlanders ignored their culture, their history, their roots.

He felt a stab of pain in his gut, as if he had been kicked.

So much effort had gone into the original mask. So much time and energy. It was charged – *he* had charged it. And then simplified for the newer, younger, forgetful, and *disrespectful* generations.

He needn't have worried.

The smallest boy shrieked out of the changing rooms, bouncing off one late market guest and into another, giggling as his friend, arms raised, and roaring chased him through the crowd.

He was wearing the mask.

"He's wearing it."

The shoppers parted, calling out for the two boys to slow down, calling for their parents to take better care of them. Stall owners cursed as the boy in the mask careened into one stall, toppling a stand of necklaces, before crashing into the next.

The smaller boy stopped, the last giggle and shriek fading from his lips, as his cheeks flattened and the pinch and flush of his skin paled. His friend, his *masked* friend, staggered between the stalls, huffing, pressing his hands to his face, only to have his fingers slide off the mask without grasping it. He dropped to his knees, then fell flat on his face, drawing a scream from his friend, and a sudden rush of people crowding the boy, and then retreating as someone took charge, ordering them to give him room, to stand back, to call an ambulance.

He watched.

The tingling surged into something less discreet, and he tugged at the hem of his parka, pulling it down, covering his excitement, as a woman kneeling beside the boy removed the mask. He gasped alongside the onlookers, gasped at the bubbles of snot, spit, and blood on the boy's lips. The crowd took a step back as the woman leaned over the boy, pinching his nose as she tilted his head back, lowering her face to his.

He took a step forward, eyes wild inside his parka, as he watched the woman blow air into the boy's mouth.

She could save him. She was *trying* to save him.

He glanced at the mask, wondering if he had charged it enough, if it had sufficient power to do the job.

He needn't have worried.

The woman rocked back onto her heels, gagging, spitting, wiping at her mouth with the back of her hand, asking again for help, then shouting for someone to call an ambulance.

Ataasinngorneq

Monday, 7th December 2043

Chapter 7

It was too early to think rationally, too dark to see clearly, but Petra struggled to believe she was going to get any sleep before her morning alarm. She slid her hand under the pillow and pulled her phone into her palm. She pressed the screen to her chest, wary of pushing the start button, or even swiping the screen to unlock the phone. It didn't matter anyway, she mused. She had seen it a hundred times already. And a hundred more in her mind. She ran through the video one more time, drawing little comfort, aware too that it only brought her more pain, just when she thought she was moving on.

Piitalaat... Don't.

"No, David. Not now. Don't tell me what I can and can't do. Not when you came back to me."

It's not me.

"How can I know that?" Petra tuned Maratse's voice out of her mind, focusing instead on his image in the video.

The camera shot was steady, barely a flicker, as if the person holding it was resting on something, or maybe even using a tripod. The background was lit with a late summer light, soft, shadow on the distant mountains across the fjord, turning the granite peaks red and gold. The image was grainy, but not too grainy to hide the buzz of mosquitoes or the wrinkles in the corners of the old men's eyes – fishermen, she guessed – as they flashed toothy grins at someone just out of shot.

Piitalaat…

The video had no sound, but Petra could hear the clump of Maratse's boots on the pebble beach as he stepped into view. She saw the arm of his jacket, the same police jacket hanging in the hall of her apartment, not two metres from where she lay.

She caught her breath, knowing what was coming next. She pressed her phone to her chest, as if she could turn the screen off in her mind, but it played on, just as the young man stepped into view.

The video was timeless; the colours of then and now matching a seascape painting, the kind one found in a museum, hues of browns, yellows, and dark grey. But not the young man. He wore his age well, clearly, a youthful grin, thick, *thick* hair, black, licked by the wind. His eyes blistered through the grainy image, strong, brown, sucking in all the light and shining, focused like a beam on Maratse.

He came next, stepping into focus, walking with deliberate steps, a smooth and steady gait, just like he always did. Petra pressed her eyes tight, but the image played on, as the young man stepped past the old fishermen, raising his hands, his arms – she saw him do it, rewinding at the same point each time as if there was a glitch in her mind as he stepped forward, throwing his arms around Maratse, turning his face towards the camera, a deep smile pinching the cheeks of his teenage face.

The video stopped then, a close-up of the young

man. But Petra turned away from his face every time, focusing instead on Maratse, the curl of his arms around the young man's shoulders, pulling him tight into an embrace, a hug.

Piitalaat…

Maratse never hugged.

At least, she couldn't remember him ever hugging anyone but her.

"He barely even smiled," she whispered, catching her own smile on her lips, curious to see if she could follow it through, if it might curl the edges of her lips. But no. The only purpose her lips served as she replayed the video over and over, was to catch the run of tears streaming down her cheeks. There was no sound in the video, but the salt from the sea stung her lips, and again as she bit them, drawing blood, biting hard to stop the video.

Petra turned her face into her pillow, wiped her tears across the cotton case, before pushing herself out of bed. She ran cold water in the bathroom sink, splashing her face, looking up, seeing the young man in the mirror, until she reached for a towel.

To think there was someone out there who Maratse had hugged.

Petra snorted, splashed more water on her face, then forced herself to speak her thoughts.

"To think he loved someone enough to hug them. To think he loved someone as much as he loved me."

She looked into the mirror, staring past the young man, challenging herself to look into her own eyes so that she might glimpse the spark of jealousy, embrace it, own it, and then *do something with it.*

"If it's real, then he's real."

Piitalaat.

"No, David. You can't help, because that voice – your voice – in my head…" She pressed her hand to her chest as she took a breath. "That voice is me. *You* know no more than me." Another breath, a rattle in her chest. "How could you?"

How could I know, or…

"That's the real question. Isn't it?"

Petra folded the towel into a square by the sink. She padded into the kitchen, sat at the table, and slid her arms onto the surface. The first sounds of the neighbours stirring in the apartment above thumped through the ceiling. Petra ignored them. She pressed her palms flat on the table, then pressed *play* one more time in her mind.

"Who is he?"

Petra paused the video long enough to get ready for the day ahead, choosing to face the brisk Arctic wind spinning drifts of snow between the parked cars as she waited for her assistant, than the stifling heat of her apartment. She let the wind blow the loose strands of her hair, resisting the urge to tuck them behind her ear, or even to pull a thin fleece hat onto her head. The wind's teeth were sharp enough to distract her, clearing her head as Constable Tiiu Mikkiki pulled into the parking lot.

"Before we go anywhere," Petra said, as she climbed into the passenger seat. "I want to apologise."

"Ma'am?"

Petra closed the passenger door and turned in her seat to face Tiiu. The look on the young constable's face brought the beginnings of a smile to Petra's lips, and she nurtured it, just as the creases on Tiiu's forehead deepened.

"Petra Jensen," she said, holding out her hand. "Your *somewhat-distracted* police commissioner."

"Constable Mikkiki," Tiiu said, grasping Petra's hand in a tentative grip.

"And where are you from, Tiiu?"

"I'm from Nuuk." Tiiu dropped her hands into her lap. "With a few years in Denmark, between Gymnasium and the Academy."

"How many did you graduate with?"

"We started with seven and ended with four."

"What year?"

"I finished PG3 two years ago and spent my first year in Sisimiut."

"But you moved back to Nuuk…"

"When Inspector Danielsen suggested it." Tiiu looked at Petra and said, "He thought we would be a good fit."

"Are you also easily distracted?"

"No, Ma'am," Tiiu said, biting her lip as she realised how it must sound. "At least…"

"No apologies, Constable." Petra smiled a little longer than necessary, hoping that it might help Tiiu relax, before checking her phone. "I want to stop off at the sports hall on the way in to the station."

"The one by the art gallery?"

"That's the one."

Tiiu put the SUV in gear and pulled out of the parking lot. "I read Sunday's report. Something about a boy being poisoned?"

"We'll know more when we get there."

"Inspector Danielsen is working the case."

"Good," Petra said. She leaned back in her seat, fastened her seatbelt and closed her eyes for a moment, opening them the second the video played. "Tell me about your family, Tiiu."

"Really?"

Petra turned her head to one side. "Really."

"Okay."

Tiiu settled into the drive and relaxed into what Petra soon understood was the constable's default chatty mode. Petra let the tales of siblings wash over her, amazed at how much Tiiu could pack into the short drive from her apartment in Qinngorput to the sports hall. Tiiu parked between two police patrol cars, promising to tell Petra more whenever she wanted, as she made sure the heating coils for the battery were turned on, before following Petra inside. Inspector Danielsen met them at the door.

"There's not much to see," he said, as he led the way between the stalls.

Petra turned her head from one side to the other as the stall owners packed their wares. The subtle blend of Sunday's narwhal curry and cinnamon stirred in the space between the aisles, reminding Petra of how much Maratse had enjoyed the markets at Christmas, how much the crafts on sale reminded him of his old hunting grounds to the north and to the east. He had sacrificed so much to be with her in Nuuk, to follow Petra's career. She struggled at times to understand why.

You know why, Piitalaat.

"Commissioner," Danielsen said.

"I'm okay," Petra said, with a nod to the cordoned off area ahead of them. "Is this where he died?"

"*Aap*." Danielsen tugged his phone from his pocket and scrolled through his notes. "His name was Niilsi Ignatiussen. Nine years old. His mother lives in Maniitsoq. He was visiting his grandparents."

"Father?"

"Deceased," Danielsen said. "Fishing accident."

"And the grandparents? You've talked to them?"

"Briefly, but not in person. I sent a unit over to the hospital. I have a constable with them now."

"Okay," Petra said, as they reached the blue and white police tape. "Talk me through it."

Danielsen described the eyewitness accounts of the boy chasing his friend between the stalls before collapsing on the floor inside the taped area.

"He was wearing a mask," he said.

Petra frowned. "Like a Christmas mask?"

Danielsen flicked through the photo album on his phone and turned the screen towards Petra. "This one," he said.

Petra took Danielsen's phone and enlarged the photo with a swipe of her finger and thumb. "It looks traditional," she said. "Thoughts?"

"More like theories, actually." Danielsen took his phone and pointed at the centre of the mask. "It's plastic, like a cheap mask the kids wear for Fastelavn or Halloween."

"Have you ever?"

"Seen anything like it?" Danielsen shook his head and lowered his phone. "Not in the stores. Apart from the stuff for Halloween. Thin masks with elastic. I think this was thicker."

"You haven't seen it?"

"It's with forensics. In the lab."

"DNA?"

"Hopefully," Danielsen said. "First, they're testing for poisons. According to his friend, Niilsi was fine until he put the mask on and started running. They found the mask in the changing rooms."

Petra turned to look toward the changing rooms, as Danielsen checked his watch. She turned back as he sighed.

"Something wrong?"

"I had an appointment," he said. "I'll reschedule."

"Can you send me the photo?"

Danielsen swiped the screen of his phone, minimising the photo and dropping it into a folder marked *Commissioner*. "Done," he said, slipping the phone back into his pocket. He gestured to a spot further away with more space between the aisles and started walking towards it. "There's more to this," he said, lowering his voice as Petra joined him.

"Explain."

"Yesterday was the second Advent Sunday this Christmas season."

"Yes?"

"We found the bodies of two older men in the same apartment block on Tuesday. Both of them died because of poisoning."

"What kind?"

"I'm waiting for confirmation, but it affected their respiratory system. The boy," Danielsen said, with a nod to the spot where he had died, "also died from respiratory failure. If there was poison on the mask, then he would have inhaled it while running. The faster he ran…"

"The harder he would breathe."

"He was chasing his friend." Danielsen looked down for a moment as he shuffled his feet. "There was a woman. She tried to resuscitate the boy, but her lips burned when she came in contact with his mouth. She had to give up."

"You think the poisoning incidents are connected?"

"I wouldn't have, if it wasn't for the day."

"Advent Sunday," Petra said.

"The *second* Advent Sunday." Danielsen lowered his voice to a whisper. "The men died on the first Advent."

"You said you found them on Monday?"

"We found them on Monday, but the doctor determined that the time of death was roughly twenty-four hours earlier."

"Three deaths through asphyxiation."

"*Aap*."

"Both traced to Advent Sundays." Petra raised her finger before Danielsen could speak. "Don't jump to conclusions, Inspector. So far, what you've got are coincidences."

"Convincing coincidences, Commissioner. I was thinking about last Christmas."

"You shouldn't. That was something different altogether. Greenland is independent now. Nothing can stop that process. There's nothing to derail, through terror or otherwise."

"We agree, but I can't stop thinking about it."

Petra felt her hands shake and stuffed them into her pockets. She had spent much of the previous December under close guard, because of the tattoos pricked into the joins between her fingers – coinciding with the marks on a victim that had been fabricated to further complicate the investigation.

"I won't sit this one out," she whispered, her lips barely moving.

"Ma'am?"

"I said, Aqqa, that I won't be pushed out of the loop on this one. If, and it's a big *if*, there is cause to believe we have another Christmas campaign, I won't be hidden away."

Danielsen grunted, and said, "I don't remember you staying out of the way, Ma'am."

"Regardless," Petra said, fixing Danielsen with a firm look. "I want regular updates. This might not be what we think it is."

"But the mask…"

"Might not be what *you* think it is." Petra waved to Tiiu and waited for her to join them. "Tiiu," she said, handing her her phone. "There's an image of a mask in my download folder. Send yourself a copy and find me an expert on Greenland masks."

"Yes, Ma'am."

Petra turned back to Danielsen. "Focus on the forensics, and where the mask came from. Tiiu and

I will look into the significance of the mask."

"You have enough on your plate, Commissioner."

"You think so? Hmm. And that's why you gave me an assistant. Well, I intend to make use of her." Petra smiled as Tiiu returned her phone. "I'm still a police officer, Aqqa, and I need a distraction from paperwork." She paused for a breath, as she fought the urge to tell Danielsen about the video. He knew Maratse, she wanted to know what he thought of it.

Not yet, she thought. *Not until I know it's real.*

"There is one more thing," she said. "And the only reason I'm telling you is because you have spies who would tell you anyway, even if I didn't."

"Spies?" Danielsen frowned.

"At the prison."

"*Naamik*," he said, with a shake of his head. "You can't visit Natuk."

"I can, Inspector, and I will."

"But why? She can't be trusted, and you can't trust her to help you with this case. And even if she could…"

"Masks, Aqqa. She used masks too, remember?" Petra pressed her hand lightly on his arm. "*You're* going to have to trust *me*."

"I do, but…"

"And," she said, pressing just a little harder. "Understand that I'm telling you as a courtesy. Something between colleagues, and friends."

"Friends?"

"Yes." Petra sighed as she let go of Danielsen's arm. "I'll tell you more when I can. But until then." She gestured at the scene of the incident behind them. “Let’s keep this quiet. No comment to the press. The investigation is ongoing. And not a word about coincidences to the First Minister. We don’t need to politicise this.” Petra turned to Tiiu, and said, “Ready, Constable?”

“*Aap*,” she said, although the return of the frown on her forehead made Petra wonder.

Marlunngorneq

Tuesday, 8th December 2043

Chapter 8

The third time he stumbled past the drunks outside the supermarket they called him over, tugging at his parka as he joined them, shaking their heads at how thin it was. He used to think it was warm, but the drunks' comments did little more than confirm what he had been thinking since he left the market on Sunday, that he should have gone home already. He hadn't gone home, and neither had he stopped walking – he needed to move to keep warm.

Sunday night had been the worst, once the excitement of the kill had drained out of him. But bad timing had left him with nowhere to go, as the excitement tapered off just as the last of the late-night shops closed. He should have gone home then but couldn't.

Too soon, he had thought, stuffing his hands deeper into his thin pockets.

The first convenience stores opened at six on Monday morning, and he had spent a fistful of change on coffee and a burger – the kind you put in a microwave. The burger bun – hot and wet – burned his fingers, but not enough to stop him buying a second in the next convenience store halfway across the city.

It was in the second convenience store he had seen the news. It had taken the police forty-eight hours to find the dead men in their apartments. The report should have given him a thrill, a shock even, but instead he experienced a wave of calm and relief, peeling the cellophane from his burger, punching the buttons on the microwave, watching the burger turn on the plate, focusing on the forty-eight hours. If he could survive forty-eight hours with nothing happening, surely he could survive forever? The thought lingered, and he chewed it over as he chewed his burger.

The city centre was small enough that he could do a circuit inside of an hour, and the snow deep enough that he recognised his tracks. He amused himself for most of the long night by pressing the thin tread of his boots into the same prints each time he passed them. The discovery of other prints and the double track of pram wheels cutting across his path had given him pause, standing there, staring, as Monday morning workers peeled around him, cursing him for the drunk they thought he was.

Not drunk, just tired and cold, he thought, once he had overcome the shock of disturbed prints.

He spent much of Monday in the public library, poring over Greenland's history, stacking the books on his table, oblivious to the looks people cast in his direction as he muttered and nodded while thumbing the pages back and forth and back again. He lingered over the images of masks, tracing the edges with his fingers, before gripping an imaginary knife, or the smooth handled gouger, working the blades in the air above the pictures as he saw the mask in his mind, as he gave it life and power.

The mask.

He caught the gasp in his throat as he dropped the invisible gouger, clapping his hand over his mouth as he remembered he had left the mask in the printer.

Always… I forget something.

He lowered his hand to his lap. Rocking gently as he thought things through. He had the only key. The only men who used the workshop were dead. That thought made him smile – light relief, but portentous, as he considered the power of the mask.

The mask could look after itself.

It was the eight remaining printed masks in his apartment that needed him. They were powerless. He should go home and charge them.

Not yet.

He turned back to the books, confident that the mask was safe, that no one would find it. But if they did, the mask could take care of itself. It said so, in the books.

The shaman destroyed his mask after use. But this was a waste. So much power, wasted. No, better to give the mask pride of place, somewhere it could be seen.

Like the masks in the book, he thought, thumbing through the colour plates, pausing over the masks with human teeth and hair. He imagined a gallery of masks, each in their own special display case, sealed but all-seeing. Visible, victorious, imbued with power and magic – *his* magic. He flicked through the pages, curious at the mention of human teeth – a child's teeth, used in powerful *tupilaq* when created to defeat one's enemies. A Greenlander, he read, employed a shaman to create a *tupilaq* for evil intent, but if the recipient after whom the *tupilaq* was dispatched allied themselves with a more powerful shaman, the magic would rebound.

It wasn't the first time he had read about rebounding magic. He paused as a familiar tingle of energy sparked through his body. To *not* destroy the mask was to flirt with dark magic. It was the ultimate test – another tingle, more sparks, from the tips of his fingers to the very ends of the hair on his head.

If I don't destroy the mask...

He replayed the scenario over in his mind, nodding as he imagined his power to be so great as to take on *all* the masks at once. Once they were charged with his magic, released into the world, only a more powerful shaman could use that magic against him. Until then, the masks were free to roam, to cause more pain and more destruction to anyone foolish enough to touch them, wear them – to *inhale* them, licking his magic from the back of the mask, drinking it deep until it was so deep, so dark, it was all-consuming.

He would consume them one by one.

Nine masks, to purge the crimes committed against him.

The order didn't matter, but a slow smile of satisfaction spread across his lips as he savoured the fact that the youngest was the first.

He could still remember the day they chased him, the boys in the playground, jeering at him, shouting his name as they pursued him across the ice outside the school entrance. There was a smooth patch of granite, curved like a whale's back. It was packed with snow, but he had hoped to reach it, so he might stand at the top, and turn and roar at the boys chasing him, stopping them with the power of his voice alone. His fists were too small to be of any use. But his voice…

… had been muffled in snow. Stifled as the boys stuffed snow in his face, filling his mouth, his ears, covering his eyes, plugging his nose. They had clamped his tiny fists to his side, pressed their knees on his chest, covered him with snow, and buried him in the drift below the granite whale's back.

They thumped him as they left him, peeling away, their jeers obscured by the snow, leaving him to claw the snow from his mouth to breathe.

Only he didn't.

I couldn't.

He rested his elbows on the desk, dug his fists into his thin cheeks, as he closed his eyes, remembering. Seeing the bright lights above him as the doctor pressed his eyes open. Feeling the trickle of snow melt out of his ears, dribble from his nose, run down his throat – coarse with grit.

"He nearly suffocated," they said.

"Open his airway."

He gagged as he remembered the tube, pushing past his teeth, turning to force his tongue flat before going further, tipping into his throat.

Perhaps he wasn't meant to feel anything, see anything, or even hear them talk, but he did. He heard what the boys had done, as the teacher related the incident from where he stood at the back of the room.

"They tried to drown him," he had said.

"They nearly did."

Drowning.

Suffocating.

He knew how it felt, but to see it… that was something else, something cathartic. It could heal him.

"Nine times."

He caught his breath as he spoke aloud, looking up, looking around, curling his fingers into fists, before leaving the table and the books, fleeing the library.

The streets were dark when he left the building. He gathered the last of the change in his thin pockets, bought a hot chocolate, then began his circuit of the city, not ready to go home. There was work to do in his apartment, more masks to be charged. He bought another hot chocolate, warmed his hands around it as he trudged a new path in the snow, curling his way around the shops, down the main street, over the hill by the old *TelePost* building, curving up and over the hump in the street before starting his descent to the docks and the older of the two hospitals: Dronning Ingrid's.

He made the hot chocolate last as he recalled what he could remember from the books, how the shaman's *tupilaq* was more powerful if something human was incorporated into it. Masks, he mused, were the same. All those masks in the books – many of them with human teeth pressed into the hole cut for the mouth. He had made a template, and it worked. *His* magic worked. But the printed masks needed charging. Without his magic, they were powerless.

They were *just* masks.

He tossed the empty paper cup into the trash and kept walking, through the dark afternoon, into the darker evening, trudging into the black night.

He could add to the masks. Take the template and enhance them.

He paused as he walked past the city cemetery.

Teeth from a dead child.

He pressed his tongue into the bottom of his teeth. He pressed hard, biting, drawing blood, enough to fuel him for another circuit as he thought about teeth and hair, but mostly teeth – *from a dead child.*

It was one of the last circuits when the drunks called him over. They said he looked lost, which confused him, that he looked cold, to which he agreed, and that they had *just the thing*, which they did. The spirits burned in his throat, licked at the lining of his stomach with a wave of barbed tongues. He took another swig when they encouraged him, and then felt bad when they told him to stop, to share, to remember his place.

Was this his *place*?

He shook his head free of the firewater. He drank in the cold air, infused with the need to return, to continue to his work and to *improve* upon it.

Teeth. The teeth of a dead child.

He would need to glue them in. The thought made him laugh – jumping to problem number two, without even considering the first problem – the more problematic of the two.

A child's teeth.

"Where are you going?" the drunks asked, as he refused another slug of spirits.

"Home."

"You have a home?" They swapped confused looks, shadow-creased as they peered at him under the streetlights. "You've been walking the streets for two nights."

"*Aap*," he said. "And now it's time to go home."

He couldn't articulate the need for penance, or his theory he had that even if it was not destroyed, if the mask's magic did not rebound within forty-eight hours, then it was unlikely that it ever would.

He walked back to his apartment, dragging his feet the last hundred metres, gripping the banister as he climbed the stairs, coughing his way through the teenagers' smoke, thinking about children's teeth as they heckled him all the way to his apartment door.

Were teenagers children?

He supposed they were, then turned the key in the lock, gagging as he entered the apartment.

It smelled of swimming pools.

His eyes smarted in the air as he tramped snow into the floor, holding his breath as he entered the kitchen and screwed the cap back onto the industrial-sized bottle on the kitchen table. He opened the window, brushing the snow from the counter as it blew in from the windowsill.

"I'm always forgetting something," he said, weary now, ready for bed.

It was time to sleep, to recharge before charging his masks.

Pingasunngorneq

Wednesday, 9th December 2043

Chapter 9

At a nod from Petra sitting in the passenger seat, Tiiu clicked the volume control on the steering wheel, filling the cab of the police SUV with the talk show host's energetic catchphrase: *Kaapi. Kaapi. Happy!* Kaapi Samøssen's light, slightly feminine voice painted a smile on Tiiu's lips and a subtle frown on Petra's forehead.

"He's really good," Tiiu said, slowing into a roundabout. "*Anaana* loves him, I mean she *really* loves him. Listens to him all the time."

Petra followed Tiiu's chatter with a dip of the head here, a raised eyebrow there, cutting through her assistant's words to tune into Kaapi's radio show. She thought of Qitu Kalia, lamenting his sabbatical year, the void it had left in the media for the likes of Kaapi Samøssen to get a foothold with little or no objective resistance. Petra had to accept, however, no matter how irritating it might be, that Kaapi had captured the heart and interest of a surprising number of Greenlanders. He spoke *to* them, and, with a subtle blend of Greenlandic, Danish, and even English, he included them all. The youngest politicians had endorsed him. He had been courted by the business sector, and even scored a series of exclusive interviews with Pipaluk Uutaaq as she steered the country into independence, transitioning from First to Prime Minister of Greenland. Through Kaapi Samøssen, Pipaluk had the ear of the people, something her father, Malik Uutaaq, had tried to get many times over the course of his political career, with varying degrees of success.

"Ma'am?"

Petra looked up as Tiiu dragged her out of her thoughts.

"He's talking about the murders."

"The murders? Plural?" Petra tuned into the radio show, curling her fingers into tight fists as she realised what Kaapi had done, and what he was about to unleash on his loyal and captive audience.

"...going to assume the killer is a *he* and say he's communicating. That's right. You heard it here, first. And I'm going to say it again, a second time. This murderer and his mask, is using our distant past to talk to us. I'm not saying that he *should* talk that way, but look at his methods, the way he kills. Just look at it – *a mask.* Right out of the past. *Bam!* He slaps us with something we have ignored for so long, something we kept on the back burner. You know? A slow heat. It's not like we didn't have a culture before we got our independence, but it was all so precious – small exhibitions in tiny galleries, a Danish documentary with Danish experts, a book published in a limited run no one can afford, or an anonymous theatre group flown all the way to New York to take part in an Expo. An *Expo*. I don't even know what that is. But I know a murder when I see one. And I saw one on Sunday. And I guarantee you're going to see more of them. This isn't a one-off. He isn't finished. He's just getting started."

"Turn it off, please," Petra said. She unclenched her fists, and then turned her palms upwards, looking at the stick and poke tattoos in the joins between her fingers, remembering the last time someone had embraced Greenland's past to terrorise Greenland's present. "How did he know about the other deaths?" she said, turning to look at Tiiu.

"Ma'am?"

"Nothing has been released about the two old men in the apartment block."

Tiiu twisted her lips to the left, dimpling her cheek as she thought. "Someone spoke to Kaapi's assistant? Called the radio, maybe?"

"And leaked important information. Who would do that?"

"I don't know." Tiiu's dimple deepened as she thought some more. "Someone with a grudge."

"Who?"

"One of the paramedics. A doctor, or maybe a police officer."

Petra turned her head to look out of the window, thinking back to the last time a police officer had used a mask to force an agenda. Only this time, the results were less likely to incite the people of Nuuk onto the streets but frighten them off them.

Tiiu pulled into the police parking lot, found a space, and switched off the engine. She sat quietly, waiting for Petra to speak.

"I need you to call Nuuk Prison – the one in Paradise Valley."

"Paradise Valley?" Tiiu said, as she pulled out her phone.

"That's what the Danes used to call it," Petra said. "We're going to visit Natuk Petersen once Inspector Danielsen has finished his briefing."

"Natuk…"

"Petersen." Petra placed a hand on Tiiu's as she made a note. "Keep it between us."

"Ma'am?"

Petra took a breath, using the brief pause to weigh her words. "Inspector Danielsen doesn't approve."

"I remember. From the sports hall."

"You have good hearing," Petra said. "Set it up, and I'll meet you back here."

Petra waited for Tiiu to nod in acknowledgment and then got out of the car. She fixed her hair on the way into the police station, stopped for a quick chat with the officer on duty in the front office, and then made her way to the briefing room. Danielsen caught her eye as she entered and then continued with the briefing.

"We've identified the poison as chlorine," he said, holding up a transparent evidence bag with a thick seal at the top. He pinched the mask inside between his fingers and thumb. "The chlorine was painted on the inside with a rubber paint. The killer…"

"The phantom at the opera," said an officer in the middle row.

Danielsen shot him a hard look, before continuing where he had left off. "… probably mixed the paint himself."

"Assuming it's a man," said another officer.

"That's what we're assuming, but without DNA." Danielsen shrugged, and said, "Whoever they are, they're being careful. Letting the victims – the boy, at least – pick up the murder weapon. It's smart. Sophisticated. It's like an invisible touch. It might even be hard to prove an actual murder took place. But we'll find them. They're in the city, and we can narrow the list of suspects down to the one thing we know for sure."

"Chlorine," said an officer at the back.

"Exactly. I want you to follow up on sales of chlorine, or even chlorine that has gone missing from stores. Liquid pool chlorine is a good bet, so I want someone to check on the swimming pool." Danielsen dropped the mask onto the briefing pulpit beside him. "Check cleaning companies – maybe they buy in bulk, mixing their own cleaning products. I don't know for sure. Just use your imagination. Be creative but be vigilant. Now that Happy Kaapi made the killer into a celebrity." Danielsen shot another look at the officer in the middle row. "You can be sure everyone will be talking about him. Get out there and get busy. We're not letting this become another Calendar Man. And," he said, glancing at Petra, "I want to remove any association with Natuk Petersen. If the people of Nuuk think she can reach out from behind prison bars, then they'll start to question security, start to question us, and before you know it, some guy is robbing a convenience store in a Santa suit."

A ripple of laughter spread through the ranks, punctuated by comments such as *that was last week,*

Inspector and *Santa's too fat to run away* as Danielsen ended the briefing.

Petra slipped out of the room before he had a chance to talk to her.

The doors clicked open as the guards buzzed them through the sluice gate system of Nuuk Prison. Tiiu followed Petra into the visitation room. She stood as Petra sat down.

"I prefer to stand, Ma'am," she said, when Petra gestured to the seat beside her.

Petra nodded, and said, "What do you know about Natuk?"

"Only what I've heard." Tiiu stiffened as the guards said Natuk would be with them in three minutes. "That she is the brother of Ooqi Kleemann, otherwise known as the Calendar Man."

"Yes. She was."

"You shot him, Ma'am."

"Yes, I did."

"And after that, she – *Natuk*, tried to disrupt the independence vote. She tried to turn the people of Nuuk against the government." Tiiu paused for a breath, drawing air into her lungs, holding it to quell the tremor in her body. "You chased her across the roof, and that was when she shot your assistant."

"Aron Ulloriaq," Petra said, smiling as she remembered how he used to encourage her to eat breakfast, anticipating her needs often before she had thought of them.

"He left the force," Tiiu said, flicking her head to one side as the door opened and Natuk Petersen walked in.

Petra stood up as Natuk hobbled towards the table. She frowned at the cuffs around Natuk's wrists, and the chain linking them to the belt at her waist and the cuffs around her feet.

"Because I was a naughty girl," Natuk said, shrugging as Petra started to speak. "The doctor was going to give me a jab of something. I didn't want it." Natuk turned her head to look at Tiiu, and said, "Petra's new assistant?"

"*Aap*."

Natuk laughed. "You know what I did to the last one?"

"You're talkative today, Natuk," Petra said, gesturing for Natuk to sit and drawing her attention away from Tiiu. "Why's that?"

Natuk's chains rattled as she slid onto the seat opposite Petra. "I heard the radio. You've got bigger problems than me, now. And yet," she said, smiling. "When I heard you were coming to see me, it made me curious. I've been silent for a long time. Perhaps now is the time to talk?"

"I hope so," Petra said. "And I hope you can help me."

Natuk tilted her head to one side, raising her eyebrows: *why?*

"You heard about the mask?"

"I heard it on the radio." Natuk glanced at Tiiu. She raised her hand, pointing her finger and thumb like a pistol. She blew Tiiu a kiss as she let her thumb fall like a hammer.

"That's enough, Natuk," Petra said. She turned to Tiiu and said. "There's coffee outside. Why don't you take a break."

"Ma'am?"

"I'll be fine." Petra smiled as Tiiu hesitated, saying nothing more until she left the room. "You're not involved?"

"You think because I used a mask as a symbol…"

"Not just a symbol." Petra leaned forwards, dipping her head in front of Natuk, out of the guard's sight, lowering her voice. "You used a mask…"

"Like it was supposed to be used," Natuk said. "I didn't pervert it. I didn't kill with it."

"People died, Natuk."

"I know."

"Now they see another mask, a year later…"

"Almost. It's early December. *Mitaartut* isn't until January."

"The sixth," Petra said. "I know."

"Then don't connect the dots." Natuk snorted, letting a soft laugh slip from her lips as Petra straightened her back. "This killer of yours. Maybe he was inspired by me. But so what? He's a one-off. Someone leaked his method to the media. No one is going to put on a mask again. It's over. He's done. If that was his opening move, he's finished. One boy dead. He'll have to force the next victim to wear a mask, and that's going to leave a trace."

"Like he did with the two men," Petra said. "Possibly."

"More tentative links, *Ma'am*?"

"Danielsen thinks so."

"Ah, Inspector Danielsen." Natuk caught Petra's eye. "What would he think if he saw us now? You sharing information from the case, with me…"

"A former police officer, who just happens to have some talent."

"You've always looked out for me. However misguided. I wonder though, does Danielsen even know you're here?"

Petra waved the thought away. "It doesn't matter."

"You don't think so?" Natuk shifted in her seat as she took a long look at Petra. "There's something else, isn't there?"

"Yes," Petra said. "I need your help."

"I've given it to you. I don't know anything about this masked killer." She raised her hands as Petra started to speak. "My mistake – a killer who uses masks, maybe more than once. Either way, it's got nothing to do with me. But one thing I can tell you – I wish Kaapi Samøssen had been on the radio in January. He might have made all the difference." Natuk pointed a crooked finger at Petra. "*He's* your real problem. He's the one who could turn Nuuk in on itself. You'll have to stop him if you want to stop the killer."

Petra sat still for a minute, absorbing Natuk's words, recognising the dangers, frowning as she wondered how she was going to tackle them. Then, the *other thing* flickered into her mind, and she took a chance.

"I need your help on a personal matter."

Natuk shook her head, letting her fringe fall over her eyes. "You killed my brother, *Ma'am*. I don't have to help you."

"I didn't say you *had* to, but I would appreciate it."

"You'd appreciate it?"

"Yes."

"How much?" Natuk gestured at the walls. "How much *appreciation* can you give me? There's no way you can get me out of these walls. It would be stupid of you to try."

Petra slipped her hand into her jacket pocket and pulled out her phone. "I received a video," she said, turning the screen towards Natuk. "I need someone to look at it, tell me what I'm seeing." She pressed play.

Petra looked into Natuk's eyes as she watched the video. She saw the tiny reflection of the screen, caught the flicker of interest in Natuk's eyes, and then held her breath as Natuk reached out to touch the screen and play the video a second time.

"Well?"

Natuk looked up at Petra, and said, "It's not what I expected."

Petra clasped the phone in her hand, hiding the screen against her palm. She took a breath, held it, and then, "What I need to know…"

Natuk waited.

"You have skills, Natuk. You can see if this is fake or not."

"Ooqi would know," Natuk said, staring at Petra. "But you killed him."

"Yes. I did." Petra swallowed as Tiiu entered the room. She lowered her voice to a whisper. "But if you can put that behind you, if you can help me. I just need to know. Is it real?"

Natuk watched Tiiu approach, looked at Petra and then raised her eyebrows, the silent Greenlandic *yes*.

Sisamanngorneq

Thursday, 10th December 2043

Chapter 10

Inspector Danielsen stuffed the tails of his light blue shirt into his trousers, pressing the folds of his belly and breathing in as he tightened his belt. He reached for his dark blue sweater hanging over the side of the chair in the bedroom, pausing as Kuuka turned onto her side. The soft red light from the Christmas star hanging in the window shone on her face, blushing her cheeks. Danielsen pulled the sweater to his chest, holding it as he watched Kuuka. He checked his watch, late already. A minute more wouldn't change anything.

She would deny it, but pregnancy suited Kuuka. While some of her friends struggled with morning sickness, Kuuka had barely reacted to the early stages, suffering the changes in her body with an almost detached amusement. Danielsen had been the one to notice the most, often pointing out things that Kuuka hadn't thought of. She called him *attentive*, and, despite the demands of work, he found he wanted to be even more attentive, to the point of suffocating, and Kuuka had encouraged him to take *one more shift*, buying herself some personal time, while banking the overtime in the special account they set up for the baby.

When she started her maternity leave, still enjoying a light pregnancy and even more time to think, she had put her plans for Danielsen's promotion into a higher gear. Even in the soft Christmas light, Danielsen could almost see her mind working, calculating. And, if he didn't leave, she would open her eyes and badger him out of the door.

He checked his watch, leaned over the bed to kiss Kuuka's lips, and then padded into the hall to find his boots. He started the car just three minutes later, pulling out of the parking space in front of their apartment, five minutes and forty seconds later than planned.

"The First Minister doesn't like to be kept waiting," Iista Enoksen said as Danielsen stepped through the door of the administration block of the Greenland government, just a stone's throw from Nuuk Police Station. Iista tugged at the hem of her cardigan and straightened her back, giving herself another two, possibly three centimetres in height. Danielsen gritted his teeth to hide his smile as he imagined that Iista would no doubt think that the possible *third* centimetre was worth the effort. "But you're in luck," Iista said, pointing a manicured nail at the door to the elevator. "The First Minister is also delayed this morning. She told me to put you in her office, and that she will be along shortly."

Danielsen followed Iista to the elevator, and, once inside and the doors closed, he said, "Kuuka says 'hi'."

Iista relaxed as the elevator started to move. She smiled, adjusted her glasses, and then whispered, "Tell her 'hi' back," just as the elevator stopped and the doors opened.

Danielsen suddenly understood that Iista was doing a favour for a friend and decided to say nothing more. He followed Iista to Pipaluk Uutaaq's office, helped himself to a coffee and found a seat. Iista promised him he wouldn't have to wait long, then left Danielsen alone, giving him more than enough time to look around the First Minister's office. She caught him standing and staring at a portrait of a man hanging on the wall when she arrived.

"That's *ataata*," she said. She hooked her winter jacket onto the stand behind the door, and then walked across the wooden floor, heels clicking, until she stood beside Danielsen. "Malik Uutaaq. Did you ever meet him, Inspector?"

"*Naamik*." Danielsen placed his cup and saucer on Pipaluk's desk, before shaking her proffered hand. "Not to speak to. But I have seen him. Before he died." Danielsen sighed and said, "Obviously."

"Don't worry, Inspector," Pipaluk said. She withdrew her hand from his, leaving a light scent of perfume on his skin. "I have come to terms with my father's death. It's his legacy I'm interested in now. He fought so hard for Greenland, often in vain, sometimes ridiculed." Pipaluk waved the thought away, fixing Danielsen with a thoughtful curve of her lips and clear, playful eyes. "More coffee? Or shall we get straight to it?"

Danielsen coughed and shuffled his feet. He wanted to look at Pipaluk, tell her he was ready to talk, but struggled to look her in the eye. Unlike Iista, Pipaluk seemed unconcerned about her height, heels or no heels. She wore clothes that Kuuka might only dream about, clothes that fit snugly, with the occasional designer wrinkle, on a body that Danielsen imagined required at least an hour in the gym every day. He sucked in his gut, did his best to look into her dark hazel eyes and nod, just once.

"Good," she said, gesturing for him to sit. "Let's begin."

Pipaluk teased her bobbed hair as she sat down, then settled her hands on her desk, waiting for Danielsen to speak. He took a quick breath, wondering where to start, and thinking that Kuuka would probably be better suited to this kind of conversation than he was.

"It's her idea," he muttered, barely aware that he had spoken.

Pipaluk dipped her head. "Yes?"

Danielsen took a moment, tried a smile, and then tried again. "I've been talking to my wife."

"Kuuka? Isn't it?"

"*Aap*."

"And how is she doing? Close to term, I believe?"

Danielsen took another breath, reminding himself not to be too impressed. There was nothing the First Minister had said that she couldn't have learned from her assistant, Kuuka's friend.

And yet.

Her composure, the way she had grown into the post of leader of a truly independent Greenland. It spoke volumes as to what she had achieved, and her ambitions. It was the latter that secured Danielsen a meeting with the soon-to-be Prime Minister of

Greenland. Ambitions. His and hers. As soon as Pipaluk took the initiative, steering the conversation, it became clear to Danielsen that Kuuka was not the only one interested in his future.

"Let me help you," Pipaluk said. She stood up to pour herself a coffee, forcing Danielsen to turn in his seat as she leaned casually against the wall, taking a sip of coffee before continuing. "I'll be blunt," she said. "Then we can dispense with any pretence. You find yourself in a challenging position. And I admit I know something about it, as it is a position – a *situation*, you could also call it – that interests me. The Deputy Commissioner is indisposed. He's sick," she said, with a shrug, casual and pragmatic. "He has cancer, and it's unlikely he will return to his post."

"Ma'am," Danielsen said, with a brief dip of his head.

"I prefer you address me as First Minister, for the time being. But…" Pipaluk smiled. "Seeing as it's just the two of us, you may call me *Pipaluk*. Less formal, more intimate. Fitting for what we're discussing, don't you think?"

Danielsen paused as he searched for the appropriate response. Pipaluk beat him to it.

"We're talking about replacing Ebbe Carlsen with Deputy Police Commissioner Aqqa Danielsen. Are we not?"

"I think so."

"I *know* so, Inspector. That's why you're here. Now…" Pipaluk put her cup down on the cabinet and returned to her desk. She pulled the chair out before sitting down, creating more room to cross her legs. Danielsen kept his eyes fixed on her face, avoiding the slim fit of the First Minister's black leather trousers. "Ordinarily, the Danish police would appoint a Deputy Commissioner, but we find ourselves in the exciting, and long overdue position of making that decision ourselves. So, now that the Greenland Police falls firmly under the control of the Greenland government." Pipaluk brushed a twist of fluff from her knee. "I am excited to be in a position to make that kind of appointment. At least, to ensure that the justice department makes the right appointment. What do you think?"

"*Aap*." Danielsen swallowed and then tugged at the collar of his shirt. He tried to remember how many floors he had come up in the elevator, and if this discussion was normal *at the top*.

"Is that a *yes* you agree, Inspector? Or…"

"I agree," Danielsen said, clearing his throat. "Most definitely."

"Good." Pipaluk pulled back her sleeve to check her watch. "My next appointment is in two minutes. But Iista knows not to disturb us until you walk out of that door."

"Yes, First Minister?" Danielsen frowned, wondering what more Pipaluk wished to discuss. There would be details of the post that might need refreshing, added areas of responsibility perhaps. Kuuka would want him to ask about the salary, but the look on Pipaluk's face suggested something else. He shifted to a more comfortable position in his seat and waited.

Pipaluk paused for what felt like more than the two minutes they had remaining, and then said, "I want to ask you about loyalty." She leaned back in her seat, fixing Danielsen with her dark hazel eyes, holding his gaze until she glanced away, allowing him to breathe again before she continued. "How loyal are you to the Commissioner?"

"Commissioner Jensen?"

"That's right. Petra Jensen. It's just…" Pipaluk paused to sigh, as if looking for the words, the right approach. "I'll be blunt." She laughed. "I'm good at that."

Danielsen forced a smile onto his lips, wondering, not for the first and probably not the last time, where the conversation was headed, and if Pipaluk had been the one to plant the seed of a meeting, and not his wife after all.

"A strong Deputy Commissioner might, even in a short time, find himself in a position to replace the sitting Commissioner."

"Sitting?"

Pipaluk brushed the word away, sending another subtle cloud of perfume towards Danielsen with a gentle wave of her hand.

"Bad choice of words. I'm confusing things. What I want, Inspector…" She leaned forward. "What I need to know is that you will step up when the time is right. I need to know that you will support me when I make a suggestion, that you will back it up, with evidence, and the right comment here and there – in public."

"*Aap*?"

"I'm asking for your loyalty, Inspector. And in return…" Another wave of her hand. "I will reward you, promote you, and ensure that you have everything you are entitled to – responsibility, power – as much as you need, and financial security for you. In short, a prosperous and comfortable life for you and your family. What do you think Kuuka would say to that, Inspector?"

Danielsen rubbed his hand over his chin. He closed his eyes for a moment, pictured Kuuka in the soft light of the cramped bedroom, baking in the tiny kitchen, curling into his body on the sofa they squeezed into the lounge. Danielsen knew exactly what Kuuka would say to Pipaluk's proposal. If she had been in the room, she would have said *yes* already, several times. But Kuuka didn't know Petra Jensen like Danielsen did. She hadn't been there when Petra went missing in Uummannaq, or when she was recovering, alone, while Maratse was in prison. She didn't know Petra like Danielsen did.

How could she, he thought, as he avoided Pipaluk's eyes.

"Inspector?"

Our baby is going to change everything – Danielsen's words, Kuuka's voice. He knew just as well as Kuuka that their tiny apartment was no place for a baby. It was barely big enough for two adults. The waiting list for accommodation was long – longer than he could remember it ever being in Greenland. But a new position, a *senior* position, perhaps even a position at the top.

It would change everything.

Loyalty was one thing, but what about the rumour that Petra was thinking of early retirement? Danielsen frowned as he tried to remember who had said it. He knew it was around the time of Maratse's funeral. It made sense, of course it did. In fact, he mused, he could even do her a favour. If he supported the First Minister's proposals, her political scheming, he might not even have to worry about being disloyal to Petra.

Not disloyal, he thought, with a shake of his head. *More like compassion.*

"Inspector? Did you just shake your head?"

"What?" Danielsen looked up, caught the flash of irritation in Pipaluk's eyes, and shook his head, again. "*Naamik*, First Minister. I was just thinking things through."

"And?"

Danielsen took a breath and nodded. "I think Kuuka would be pleased." Another breath. "We both would."

Pipaluk stood up, extending her hand, and Danielsen pushed himself to his feet. "I'm so pleased you think so," she said. "Keep your phone close, Deputy Commissioner. You'll be hearing from us shortly."

Danielsen's face flushed as his phone rang. Pipaluk nodded for him to take it, and he took a step closer to the door, swiping the phone with his thumb to answer it. The First Minister watched him from behind her desk, giving Danielsen the impression that she heard every word.

"Is that something I should know about?" Pipaluk asked as Danielsen ended the call.

"We have a tip on a potential suspect."

"For the mask killing?" Pipaluk tilted her head for a second, as if giving Danielsen a moment to think before she said, "If we're going to work together, Inspector…"

"Yes, First Minister. It's about the mask murder."

"And you're supervising the investigation?"

"Leading it," Danielsen said.

Pipaluk sighed as she leaned back in her seat. "I'm pleased," she said. "You need to put an end to this, Aqqa, as quickly as possible. We can't have another Christmas season spoiled by a madman loose in the city."

Danielsen nodded as he thought about how to reply, how a *Deputy Commissioner* might reply. But the words failed him, and he turned quietly for the door.

"Don't let me down," Pipaluk called after him.

Tallimanngorneq

Friday, 11th December 2043

Chapter 11

Tiiu parked the patrol car at the end of *Tuapannguit*, tucking it behind a large white van. She switched off the engine and waited for a sign from Petra that they should get out of the car.

"Not yet," she said. She took a breath and ran through her reasons for taking Tiiu into the field. If nothing else, Petra knew she would be forced to click into gear, once Danielsen gave the order to make the arrest. *A good distraction,* she thought, pushing the images of the video further into the back of her mind. She nodded at the cluster of uniformed men and women grouped around Inspector Aqqa Danielsen to their right. "We'll let Aqqa finish his briefing. Meanwhile," she said, turning to look at Tiiu. "What have I missed?"

"Ma'am?"

"Well, either my calendar has been suspiciously empty of late or you haven't been given access to it. I'm quite sure Monday's budget meeting isn't the only meeting I have next week." Petra smiled, and said, "Not that I'm complaining, but if I had known this was going to be a light week, I might have scheduled a few meetings myself."

Petra waited as the young police constable fidgeted in the driving seat. The look in her eyes, the furtive glances she cast through the window, together with the uncharacteristically quiet car journey from the station to the location of the arrest, suggested that there might be a good reason Petra's calendar had been purged of meetings.

"Tiiu?"

"I'm sorry, ma'am," Tiiu said, casting another furtive glance at Danielsen. "It's all moving so fast. I feel like I'm in over my head."

"It's okay," Petra said. She lowered her voice, softening her tone as she studied Tiiu for more clues – the sweat marks from her palms on the steering wheel, the fact that she hadn't stopped twitching since parking the car. "You can tell me. I won't be mad."

Tiiu turned to look at Petra, catching her eye, before gulping air into her lungs and then talking, the words gushing out of her mouth in one big release.

"I was told to keep your calendar light, to postpone meetings that could wait until January, and to cancel others that were unnecessary."

"I see."

Tiiu swallowed before continuing.

"I didn't decide what was unnecessary. I wouldn't do that – *couldn't* do that. I was just following orders. That's all."

Tiiu clamped her lips shut and held her breath. The few looks she cast at Petra were subdued, head down, with little or any light reflecting in her eyes, despite the midmorning sun and the blanket of reflective snow on the ground.

"You were following orders."

It wasn't a question, but Tiiu nodded anyway.

"Danielsen's orders?"

Tiiu nodded.

Petra turned, and said, "I won't bite, but I need to hear you say the words, Constable."

"*Aap*," Tiiu said. "Inspector Danielsen told me what I should do."

"He told you specifically?"

"We went through your calendar together."

"When?"

"Yesterday. I had an evening shift – some overtime. He came by the office after his meeting with the First Minister."

"Pipaluk," Petra said, with a sigh. "Of course."

"Ma'am?"

"Don't worry about it, Tiiu." Petra reached out to take Tiiu's hand. She grasped the young constable's fingers, squeezed once, and then said, "Let's go and see what's going on, shall we? The rest can wait."

"You won't say anything to Inspector Danielsen?" Tiiu's hand twitched as Petra let go of her fingers.

"Not today," Petra said. "At least not until we've caught our killer." Petra opened the passenger door. "You can fill me in on the details as we walk."

Petra got out of the car and turned her collar up. The wind blowing in off the sea curled clouds of ice crystals from the roofs of the smaller shops and offices dotted around the approach to the apartment block. She zipped her jacket to her chin and stuffed her hands into her pockets, nodding for Tiiu to catch up as she walked towards Danielsen and the group of police officers doing one last equipment check.

"His name is Miilu Bendtsen. He's twenty-nine years old, and lives in apartment 22C on the third floor."

Tiiu fell into step alongside Petra as they followed Danielsen and his team towards the main entrance of the apartment block. The team of eight officers split into three, with two teams of three peeling off from the main group to jog around the sides of the block, while Danielsen followed the two remaining officers inside.

"We'll wait here," Petra said, as she slowed to a stop at the end of the path leading to the main entrance. "Keep talking, Constable."

"Okay," Tiiu said, with a nod of her head. "Miilu works at the swimming pool. He's a lifeguard. But he's also responsible for cleaning the pool and adding chlorine to the water." Tiiu shrugged when Petra looked at her. "I don't know how they do it, but it's the fact that he has access to chlorine that brought us here."

"Not only that, surely?"

"*Naamik*." Tiiu paused as the radio clipped to her collar crackled into life.

Each of the teams reported in to say they were in position. Petra tilted her head to one side to listen as the team at the rear of the building was the last to report in. She pictured each team in her mind, imagining Danielsen to be at Miilu's door, while the team at the rear would stop him leaving the apartment. The third team at the side of the building covered the emergency exits and the fire escape. A flurry of snow curling off the top of the apartment block drifted down to the ground, obscuring Petra's vision for a moment as she stared at the main entrance, the front door, wondering who, apart from her and Tiiu, had that covered.

"What really makes him interesting," Tiiu said, continuing with her report, "is that his boss, at the swimming pool, said he hadn't seen Miilu for three days."

"He's sick?"

"If he is, he didn't call it in."

"A girlfriend then?"

"Boyfriend, or acquaintance – we're not sure. But we know his friend lives in the same apartment block."

"What floor?"

"Ah…" Tiiu checked her phone. "Second," she said, after swiping her finger across the screen to access Miilu's file on the secure server.

"And Miilu? Remind me?"

"He lives on the third floor," Tiiu said.

Petra brushed more snow from her hair, then tucked a loose strand behind her ear. She glanced at Tiiu's utility belt, at the pistol holstered just above her right hip. Her own hips were noticeably unhindered, free of weight, and Petra sighed as she realised she was wholly unprepared for any unforeseen developments, such as…

"Going in on three."

Danielsen's voice cut through Petra's thoughts and the light but persistent wind now blowing in from the sea.

"Get ready, Tiiu," Petra said.

"Ma'am?"

Petra pointed at the front door. "We've got the back, and the side covered."

"*Aap*."

"Danielsen is going in right now."

"Yes."

"And you said Miilu has a friend on the second floor."

"Maybe his boyfriend." Tiiu shifted her feet in the snow. "I don't remember his name."

"It's not important," Petra said, pausing as Danielsen swore, passing the word that Miilu's apartment door was unlocked, but the apartment was empty. "Get ready, Tiiu."

The radio burst into life with more curses, followed by shouts indicating movement on the second floor. Danielsen followed up with the order for each team to hold position, that his team was proceeding to the stairwell. Petra almost smiled at the sound of Danielsen panting, drawing more air into his lungs as he charged along the corridor to the stairs.

"Go, Tiiu," Petra shouted, grabbing a handful of Tiiu's jacket above her right shoulder, and thrusting her forward, along the path to the main entrance. Miilu burst out of the front door a second later, skidding in the snow as Petra and Tiiu ran towards him. "Miilu Bendtsen," Petra shouted. "Stop."

Miilu did stop, for one second, perhaps three, as he shivered in the snow, his long black hair flowing in the wind, brushing his bare chest and shoulders, before he turned away from the building and ran towards the sea.

For all her youth and nervous energy, Tiiu

lagged behind Petra as they chased Miilu across the snow, slowing as they charged through the drifts collecting on the lee side of granite blocks, before climbing up and over them. Petra looked back over her shoulder at Tiiu, saw two teams of police officers pounding around the side of the building, and then turned back to see how far Miilu had run, and to try to anticipate where he was running to. Petra slid halfway down the snow-clad granite, yanked Tiiu's radio from the clip on her jacket, and took off after Miilu.

"Commissioner," Tiiu called out. "Wait."

But Petra was gone.

Miilu left a soft trail in the snow, with small prints and no tread. Petra stared at his prints as she ran, slowing when she reached the corner of a low wooden building, smiling as she realised Miilu was barefoot. She rounded the corner, glimpsed his hair streaming behind him in the wind like a stallion's mane, then pushed on, closing the gap.

She caught herself laughing, as if after so much time behind the desk, she was suddenly free – running free.

Careful, Piitalaat.

"Not now, David," she said, between breaths. She wanted to add something about *unfinished business* and *I'll deal with you later*, but managed little more than, "I'm busy," before she followed Miilu down a steep bank of snow to a track twisting alongside the rocks, close to the sea. Petra slid after him, slowing her descent with her heels, before thudding into a rock at the bottom. The impact jarred through her heels, bringing a curse and a cry to her lips. She picked herself up, limping the first few steps, before gritting her teeth and running.

Miilu turned once to look back at Petra, shouted something in Greenlandic, then pushed on, through the snow, along the track, until he reached the curve of a tiny pebble beach, crusted with ice. Petra watched as Miilu leaped off the track, choosing the shortcut from one point of the beach to the other.

If he hadn't slipped on the ice, he might have made it.

Petra slowed as Miilu fell, catching her breath as she approached him, palms raised, loose strands of hair whipping across her face, just as Miilu's hair covered his.

"Miilu Bendtsen," she said. "Just stay there."

"I've done nothing wrong," he shouted back, switching to Danish.

"We can talk about that."

Miilu pushed himself into a crouch, tensing as Petra closed the distance between them to less than two metres. He watched Petra pick her way across the ice, waited for her to pause in front of the same flat slab upon which he had lost his footing.

"Miilu," Petra said, as he shivered into a standing position. "Think about this." She hiked her thumb over her shoulder. "You know there are more police on the way."

Miilu stared at her, then turned his head at the sound of boots thudding along the track towards them. He turned his head left, towards the sea, and then darted towards it.

"Shit," Petra said, before racing after him.

Miilu dived into the water as soon as it was

deep enough, twisting between the growlers of ice scraping the shallows. Petra felt the cold seep into her boots, tugging at her trousers, and filling her pockets as she waded in after Miilu. Her teeth chattered, and she cursed herself for being so stupid. *There's a reason so few Greenlanders swim,* she thought, as Miilu surfaced a few metres ahead of her.

"Commissioner!"

Petra thought about turning, perhaps even waving to the police officers on the beach, but as the freezing waters lapped at her waist, she ignored them, reaching instead for Miilu's arm as the sea chilled his body, and his hair hung cold and wet on his shoulders.

"Let me he…" Petra bit her lip as her body shook. "Let me help you."

Miilu slid his hand towards her, and Petra took it, pulling him back to beach, through fist-sized lumps of brash ice, past the growlers and into the arms of the police.

Arfininngorneq

Saturday, 12th December 2043

Chapter 12

The family in the apartment above woke late on Saturday, allowing Petra an extra hour of sleep. She tugged the duvet over her head and then curled the corner in her fist under her chin. She sniffed back another stream of snot, then smiled, wide eyed, staring across the bedroom, but looking beyond the walls to the sea. She lifted her legs to wrap her feet in the bottom of the duvet as she remembered the sea spilling over the collars of her boots. She imagined wading into the water, gasping as the chill crept up her body, pressing her legs like a vice, reaching higher, above her waist, to close fingers of frost around her heart.

Another sniff.

She couldn't remember the last time she had felt more alive.

Everything that had happened, or not happened through the year since chasing Natuk Petersen across the rooftops, since shooting Ooqi Kleemann in Little Chinatown, the bureaucracy of change – the transition from a self-ruling state to an independent country – it was all so tiring, draining.

So Boring.

It could have been Maratse's voice, but they were definitely Petra's words.

And yet, chasing Miilu from his apartment to

the sea – never mind if he was the killer or not – it was…

Exhilarating.

Petra had glossed over the after action report, suggesting to Danielsen that if he really wanted to admonish her for being reckless, he might have thought to leave a team at the main entrance, rather than trusting that the Police Commissioner and her assistant be the ones to watch that exit.

"Which we did," she had said, quietly, firmly. There was no need to gloat, but Petra enjoyed the subtle change in the looks the police officers at the scene had given her. She used to be active, but the past year had seen her chained to the office, and at the beck and call of the First Minister, or any minister *she* felt warranted a meeting with Greenland's police commissioner. The looks the officers gave her for an entire year were blank and remote. It felt good to see a little light in their eyes when she looked at them, something verging on newfound respect.

"Careful, Petra," she said, worming her chin deeper into the duvet until only her eyes and forehead were visible. "Don't let it go to your head."

Piitalaat…

Of course, there was still the video.

Petra rubbed her nose on the duvet, pulled it to one side, and then shivered her way out of bed. She pulled a thick dressing gown over her pyjamas, tugged wool socks over her feet, then, still shivering, she slid her arms inside Maratse's old police jacket, tugging it around her waist, before zipping it halfway up her chest.

"I'm still thinking," she said, glancing up and to the side, as if Maratse might be watching or listening.

The choice, so early on a Saturday, was simple. She could embrace the cold she had caught as a result of following Miilu into the black December sea, or she could watch Maratse's video for the thousandth time, wondering how Natuk knew it was real, and who might have sent it. The other question – the identity of the young man Maratse hugged in the video – was something she couldn't think of, not yet, even if she wanted to.

Petra filled the kettle with water, choosing a strong lemon and ginger tea from the cupboard, and allowing herself to be sick for a little while, to wallow in self-pity, to binge something old and nostalgic on television, and to remember what it had been like to be a young constable – Tiiu's age – if only for the first half of the day. Police work and Maratse, returned from the grave, would just have to wait.

The kettle boiled. She made tea, but stopped short of grabbing the TV remote and flopping onto the couch at a knock on the door.

"Joshua," she said, as she opened it.

"This could be a bad time," Seabloom said. "But I heard what happened, and I brought supplies." He lifted the cloth shopping bag in his hand, opening it to show Petra the items inside. "I have peanut butter, chocolate, more peanut butter..." He frowned. "Ah, that would be peanut butter *in* chocolate. Some fruit, some tea, drugs..."

"You have drugs?"

"Yes."

Petra took a step back to let Seabloom into her apartment. "You should have started with the drugs."

"I grabbed some *Tamiflu* from the dispensary on the base."

"So, *real* drugs then?"

"Yes. I suppose." Seabloom looked at Petra, tilting his head as if seeing her for the first time, or seeing something odd. "Prescription drugs. The base doctor said I could take them if I vouched for you."

"And you *vouched* for me?" Petra felt her lips crease as she tried to balance her smile, wondering whether she was flirting, wondering if she cared, or if the sudden sniff of a runny nose might make Seabloom change his mind.

And what if he did? Would I run after him, would I...

"Your jacket," Seabloom said.

Petra caught her breath, shifted gear, and plucked at the front of the jacket. "David's. I can't bring myself to get rid of it." She shrugged, releasing a wave of something she couldn't smell, but could see in the wrinkles of Seabloom's nose. "That would be essence of husky, or something like that." She shut the door and slipped past Seabloom, heading for the kitchen. "I just made tea. I'll make some more. Kick off your shoes and bring your drugs." Petra giggled as she repeated the line, curious at the sudden giddiness, deciding that she liked it, that she *liked* having a man come and visit her, especially one who brought her chocolate and drugs.

Seabloom dumped his bag onto the kitchen table, took the mug Petra offered him, and then leaned against the counter, smiling as he looked at her.

"You can stand," Petra said. "But I have to sit." She slid a finger out of the huge cuffs of Maratse's dirty jacket and pointed at the couch. "I'm going over there."

"I'll join you."

Petra curled into the far end of the couch, closest to the wall, as Seabloom settled into the opposite corner. She tucked her feet under a blanket, suddenly aware of the gap – less than a metre – between them, and curious once more about how right it felt, as if she had passed some invisible marker, after which it was okay to live and perhaps even love again. She clutched her mug to her chest, pretending that it was the tea and not some inexplicable flush of emotion that was warming her inside.

"Tell me what happened," Seabloom said. He rested his arm on the back of the couch and looked at her. Another smile. He waited.

"We thought we had him, the killer," Petra said, sliding one foot just a few millimetres closer to Seabloom. "At least, that was the hope."

"But you didn't?"

"It's not him. Miilu Bendtsen ran because he was smoking hash with his boyfriend. He'd been stoned for three days. Had missed work. Unluckily for him, he just so happened to have access to chlorine."

"Bleach?"

"Stronger," Petra said. "Chemicals for the swimming pool."

"Right." Seabloom smiled. "I always forget that Nuuk has a swimming pool. It's not the first thing one thinks about when you think about Greenlanders. Swimming, I mean. It's not like I ever imagined Greenlanders would swim."

Petra curled her lips to one side, as if contemplating swimming in the sea. "I think what I was doing was wading, not swimming. Miilu, however, he gave it a good go. A good effort. Until the cold got to him."

"The *cold got to him*? Petra," Seabloom said, reaching for her foot. "The sea around Nuuk is full of icebergs. There are growlers on the beach, brash ice clinging to the rocks. It would be like swimming at…"

"The North Pole?"

Petra glanced at Seabloom's hand as he rubbed her foot through the blanket.

"Yes," he said. "Exactly."

Petra pushed her foot free of the blanket, deeper into Seabloom's palm. She swallowed, as he continued to rub, looking at him over the lip of her mug. Seabloom put his tea down and pulled Petra's foot gently into his lap, smoothing his thumbs into the arch of her foot, brushing his skin against hers, just inside the cuffs of her pyjamas bottoms.

"We've been concerned," he said, catching Petra's eye, holding her gaze for a moment, then looking away, working his fingers over her foot, brushing his thumbs once more, then often against her skin.

"At the base?" she said. Another swallow followed by a sniff, drawing a sympathetic smile onto Seabloom's lips.

"Yep. After the Calendar Man last Christmas, then Natuk…"

"Petersen."

Seabloom looked up. "She's a dangerous woman."

"Dangerous woman or dangerous person?"

"Hmm, that feels like a trap, Commissioner."

"Maybe it is, *Commander*."

"Then I would say that she is simply dangerous. Her gender has nothing to do with it."

Petra shifted position, stretching both legs towards Seabloom, as she slid further down the couch. He lifted a leg over hers, tucking his foot between the side of the couch and Petra's bottom.

"As I was saying…" Seabloom said.

Petra swallowed for the third time, breathing slowly, soundlessly, if it wasn't for the sniffle.

"We could help out."

"I think we've got this one."

Seabloom shrugged. "It's nearly Christmas, Petra. I can put a few officers on it. Help your officers. Maybe lighten the load a little."

Petra felt the press of Seabloom's foot against her bottom – couldn't ignore it, and the gentle rubbing of her feet.

"Are you okay?" Seabloom asked, as she bunched her toes.

"Yes," she breathed. "I was just wondering

about my socks…"

Seabloom slowly peeled one sock off Petra's foot, then the other. She pressed her teeth into her bottom lip as she studied his chiselled jaw, smiled at the flecks of grey in his hair, the beginnings of his five o'clock shadow, and the way the late dawn light reflected in his grey eyes.

It's okay.

The voice gave her pause, but not enough to distract Seabloom. She sniffed, smiled when he looked at her, nodded when he made a comment about the drugs, shaking her head when he suggested he get them.

It's been a year.

Her feet cooled, but she didn't want him to stop, didn't want the socks to be a barrier between them.

It doesn't mean I love him any less.

"I'm wearing your jacket, for God's sake," she whispered.

"What's that?" Seabloom looked up.

"I was just wondering." Petra rested her head against the side of the couch, felt a strand of hair fall across her cheeks. She left it there. "I'm older than you."

"Possibly."

"No," she said. "I *am* older than you."

Seabloom moved his foot, the one Petra thought she had pinned beneath her bottom. She watched him move, shifting position. She held her breath as he took her mug gently from her hand, pausing, raising his eyebrows, then placing it on the coffee table when she nodded. She felt that same flush, the one she tried to blame on her hot tea, flaming now, filling her chest, as he leaned forward, one hand, brushing her hair from her face, teasing it to one side, as she caught her breath – another sniffle, something to make them both laugh.

"Commissioner," he said, leaning closer.

"*Commander.*"

Petra tried, she really did, but the cheesiness of the hushed titles hit her like a polar bear swatting a seal. Her body creased as she laughed, sniffing back a stream of snot, clutching Seabloom's shoulder as he pulled away, laughing again, then pulling him close, holding him at just the right distance, staring into his grey eyes. Any closer and she would turn cross-eyed. They both would.

"I'm sorry," she said. "I'm over it now. It won't happen again."

Seabloom dipped his head, then lifted it again, slightly, looking into Petra's eyes as she wrapped her hand around his neck, pulling him close.

Maratse's secret could wait.

The killer and his masks could wait.

I'm sick, and this kind man is here to help me.

She suppressed another bout of laughter as Seabloom's lips brushed hers.

And he brought me chocolate and drugs.

Sapaat

Sunday, 13th December 2043

Chapter 13

The rubber paint in the bottom of the plastic margarine tub was dry. He picked at a corner, teased and pulled it, until the end came free of the tub and he pulled it away like a flap of blue rubber skin. He flopped it onto the surface of the kitchen table, right beside the mask. Mask number two, the teacher's mask.

The year it happened was difficult to remember, as was his age, but he pictured his face – the teacher's, remembered his pale skin, the white flakes on the man's chapped lips, the red bite of cold weather prickling the skin in the corners of his mouth. The man was Danish, newly arrived, unused to the cold, suffering for it, but revelling in everything. He had time for all the kids, and he made even more time for those he liked. Perhaps their fathers were hunters, or they had a boat – access of some kind to the water. The teacher was in Greenland to learn to hunt. He didn't hide the fact. Everybody knew it, and the kids who could give him access to what he wanted were the ones he liked the best.

There were lots of *kaffemiks* in Nuuk, and he remembered going to them as a young boy, armed with a handful of Danish kroner that he would present to the birthday boy and girl at the door. The *kaffemik* was always a bittersweet experience. On the one hand, there was food and plenty of it, enough to make his stomach swell for two days afterwards. But there were lots of kids too, kids from school, kids from his apartment block. They had more money, more friends, more computer games, more clothes. Just more and more besides.

They also had more to offer the teacher.

He remembered the day after the *kaffemik*, when the teacher took the register at the start of class. When he called out the girl's name, the one who had just celebrated her tenth birthday – other people's ages were easier to remember – the teacher lingered over her name, thanking her for a fun afternoon. Everybody who was there would also remember how the teacher had spent most of the afternoon in the kitchen, his loud voice rumbling around the apartment as he plagued the girl's father with questions about calibres and distances, what sight he should buy, if he should buy a shotgun for ptarmigan, whether he would need a licence.

The Dane was a hunter trapped in a teacher's body.

He snapped out of his thoughts, fingering the mask on the kitchen table, then adjusting the strap of the face mask he wore, tapping the filter as he remembered what the teacher had said when he found him in the bathroom.

"You should be outside," he had said. "Playing with the other kids."

"They don't want to play with me."

That's when the hunter took over. He remembered seeing the change in the teachers' eyes, the moment when compassion was replaced with pity, when his pedagogy failed him and the teacher almost sneered when he looked at him, reducing him to one of the weak, the kind that were supposed to be culled from the herd.

"Then you'll just have to try harder," he said, pointing at the door and waiting for him to slide off the toilet seat and leave the bathroom. The teacher called out to him to *keep going* all the way to the outside door, until he stepped out of the school and onto the playground.

Playground. That was one word for it.

He tapped the mask again, inspected the tip of his gloved finger and smiled. It was ready.

He remembered to twist the cap back onto the bottle of chlorine, to leave the window on the hook, to press the lid back onto the paint so that it wouldn't dry out, and then he carried the mask out of the kitchen. He stopped in the doorway, dropped the charged mask into a plastic carrier bag, then hung it on the rack in the hall beside his parka. He went into the living room, walked right to his desk, and then stopped and stared at the mask lying in the middle of it.

The mask.

He traced his gloved fingers round the rough edges, felt the prick of a splinter catch in the cotton weave. He picked up the mask, turning it to look through the ragged holes he had made for the eyes. The builder's mask covering his face got in the way when he held the carved mask to his face, and he hurriedly pulled it off, muttering, "Always forgetting something."

It didn't matter. Now that his face was free, he could feel the cool touch of the mask against his skin, smell the soot that pricked at his nostrils. If he wore the mask…

The thought gave him pause. He *could* wear his own mask – not the printed ones charged with dark magic – but his own, just like the shaman of old. He could wear the mask as a disguise, with which he could pass unseen. He *had* to do something. Now that the radio host…

"Kaapi."

He spat the name.¨

… now that he had warned everyone against wearing the printed masks, no one was ever going to pick one up again. He was going to have to get close to them, to *help* them put the mask on. To do that he would need the power of the shaman, old Greenland magic, the power of disguise.

He found the lengths of cord tied into the wooden mask and pulled them tight around the back of his head, fastening the cord so that it rested on his ears. The mask squashed the tip of his nose, and he could taste the soot on his tongue as he pushed it through the mouth hole. He would have to breathe through his mouth. The nostrils were purely decorative.

He had not thought about that.

He walked around the living room, holding his hands out to his sides, moving them back and forth, testing the limits of his periphery vision. He remembered struggling with the peripheries on the playground. He tried to keep the other children in sight, searching for the bullies, only to lose sight of them as they prowled around the edges of his vision, forcing him to twist one way, and then the next, until he ran for the door, only to bump into the teacher standing in front of it.

"Go on, Josef," the teacher said. "Go and play."

Josef ran along one side of the school, coughing through the smoke of the older children as they puffed at their forbidden cigarettes. He leaped over their legs as they tried to trip him, before running fast, the wind piercing the weave of his thin jacket, cooling the thin air inside his lungs, until they caught him, from the sides – always from the sides.

"Poor little Josef," they called him, a fist for each word.

"Stupid Josef."

And then, "Bloody Josef," as his nose burst with snot and blood.

The teacher found him, helped him onto his feet, dusted his parka, and then pointed him towards the door.

"You can go inside now, Josef," he said, brushing the hand Josef tried to curl into his to one side, muttering something about him being *all bloody*.

Bloody Josef.

That's what they called him.

And he was.

Often.

But in the living room of his tiny apartment, he – *Josef,* was powerful. He was still thin, and he still suffered from nosebleeds when the temperature reached minus twenty, but he wasn't little anymore.

He removed the mask, steadying himself as he

felt a wave of giddiness wash over him. He found a second carrier bag and slid the carved mask inside it. He carried it to the front door, pulled on his parka, tugged on his boots, and then took both bags with him on his way out of the apartment. He closed the door, felt it lock with a soft *snick*, and then wondered what he had forgotten.

"Something," he whispered, and then looked at the carrier bags in his hands. It didn't matter. He had his masks – one for disguise and one to purge another memory, to make him strong as he overcame the trials that had held him back as a child. He felt the chill of the wind pressing through the thin weave of his gloves, and then walked down the stairs, pressing the air out of the snow in soft squeals beneath the soles of his boots.

He sniffed in the wind, searching for the prickle of tobacco smoke, only to smile as he realised it was the soot from the carved mask that he could smell.

Power.

He could smell it. He drank it in, letting the wind blow through his black hair as he walked to the bus stop, taking the next bus into the city centre.

The Danish teacher from Josef's school years left Nuuk two years after he had arrived, complaining about the children, the lack of discipline, the lack of collegial support, the children again, and something about not being appreciated. He never did go on the hunt, and the children in Josef's class told of how the teacher had tried to sell his shotgun to their fathers, once he realised he couldn't take it with him back to Denmark.

"You need a hunting licence to own a gun in Denmark," they said.

But not in Greenland.

Josef knew that *the* Dane was long gone. But, just as the boy in the Christmas market was not *the* boy who had chased him in school, he knew that a suitable substitute could be found, that the effect would be the same so long as the magic was strong enough.

Josef had charged the mask himself. He knew it was strong enough. Now he needed a suitable substitute.

He wandered the streets for an hour, careful to stay in the shadows, careful to avoid the drunks. When he found a Dane, it didn't matter that they were female, only that she was alone. He followed her along the pedestrian street, hushing the wind with soft whispers over thin lips as the plastic bags crackled. The woman slowed to answer a call on her phone, then turned up *Aqqusinersuaq*, along Nuuk's main street, heading for the old *TelePost* building at the top of the gentle hill, opposite the church.

He wondered if she was going to the church. It was Advent, after all.

He smiled as she crossed the street, striding now, chatting on her phone, clasping the hat on her head for fear of losing it in the wind.

She slowed as she approached the church gate, slipping her phone into her pocket as she ended the call. She walked along the dark path towards the cross of light on the side of the church – a feature and a design, drawing people out of the dark and into the light.

If they were fast enough.

Josef took out the carved mask, slipped it onto his head and stuffed the bag into his pocket. Again, the soot pricked at his nostrils, filling them as he breathed through the hole in the mouth. He took the printed mask out of its bag, stuffing that bag into another pocket as he increased speed, running now, crunching through the snow and turning the woman's head, until she spun around, startled, mouth open, poised to scream, only to have her breath clog her throat, as Josef pressed the printed mask to her face.

She gagged as he pinched the sides to her cheeks, pressing her onto the path, into the snow, as her legs buckled, and her breath bubbled in her mouth. Josef held the held the mask there, against her face, as she lay in the snow. He slipped the elastic over her head, pulling it tight, and then stepped back. He turned his head to the sides, checking his periphery vision, drinking in more soot, and then trembling at the familiar tingle in his fingers and his crotch, as his blood pumped, thumping and thudding at his temples.

He heard the click of the church door, snapped his head around and stared as someone stepped out of the church.

When they screamed, he ran.

Ataasinngorneq

Monday, 14th December 2043

Chapter 14

Petra zipped the collar of her jacket all the way to her chin as she waited for Tiiu to get out of the patrol car. The blue and white police tape snapped in the wind, twisting with flurries of snow, bowing in the middle of the longer stretches as the snow settled on it. The wind blistered their cheeks as they trudged through the snow to where Danielsen and three more police officers searched the area outside the church.

"We have a witness who said he ran that way." Danielsen pointed at the gravestones curving down towards a track running from the road and around the back of the church grounds. Residents of the apartment block opposite the church lounged on the balconies, braving the wind and the snow to watch the police at work. "If he did – and we assume he did – then the snow has already covered his tracks. But it makes sense. He can run around the back of the church, and then back into the city centre. There are no streetlights along the track."

"And none here," Petra said, turning to look at the impressions in the snow where the body lay.

"We wanted to have a look in the daylight. They moved the body late last night."

"Do we have a name?"

Danielsen checked his phone and said, "Sara

Norup. Danish. Thirty-two years old. She works for Air Greenland's tourist office." He pointed at the church. "She was coming for the Advent service after work."

"And the eyewitness?"

"Saw the man first. At least, she said it was a man. But she described the mask he was wearing as very black, but marked with lines, all the way across the face, just like the mask we found on Sara Norup's face."

"Attached?"

"With an elastic around the back of her head."

"And the cause of death?"

"We're waiting for the final report, but it looks like the same as the last one. Plus, the mask had the same blue coating on the inside. It looks like the killer is mixing his own paint and adding the chlorine."

"Okay." Petra shivered, drawing a look from Danielsen.

"I thought you were sick. Shouldn't you be at home, Commissioner?"

"I'm fine," Petra said, suppressing another shiver and the real reason she didn't want to be at home. *I need to keep busy. Too much downtime is…* She shook her head as Danielsen started talking to her, then focused on what he was saying – something about Joshua Seabloom, and the US Coast Guard's offer of help.

"They have some intelligence officers and he suggested they might be of service."

"They are concerned," Petra said, casting a furtive look at Tiiu, wondering if she knew about

Seabloom's home visit. "I don't see any problem with getting a little help from our friends."

"It might send the wrong signal," Danielsen said.

"To whom?" It took Petra a moment, and then she got it. She turned her body with the wind, feeling it press against her back as she looked at Danielsen. "You're thinking of *optics*, Inspector, is that it?"

"Optics? I don't know what you mean."

"I think you do. And I think the First Minister's got her claws into you." Petra reached out, pressing her hand against Danielsen's arm. "Be careful, Aqqa. She'll use you just as long as you are useful." Petra let go and turned to Tiiu. "Ready?"

"*Aap*," she said.

Danielsen frowned as Petra turned to walk away. "Ready for what?"

"We have a meeting with Professor Korniliu Duko, the museum director. You've done a brilliant job of clearing my calendar, Inspector. I thought I would do something useful and pick the director's brains about masks." She tucked her hands into her jacket pockets and dipped her head towards the victim's outline in the snow. "You'll keep me informed?"

Danielsen nodded and then turned away, but not before Petra caught the look in his eyes, surprising herself with an surge of sympathy as she realised she couldn't remember when she last saw the Inspector look quite so tired.

Yes, I can, she thought, as she followed Tiiu back to the patrol car. *Last Christmas.*

The stairs creaked as Korniliu Duko led Petra and Tiiu up a narrow staircase to his office. He told them to *mind their heads* as they entered the attic space, before gesturing for them to sit on two threadbare armchairs positioned at an angle like the tip of an arrow in front of the museum director's sturdy mahogany desk.

"It's the captain's desk from an old whaler," he said, as Petra and Tiiu sat down. Korniliu ran his fingers on the back of his chair as he stood in the spot that afforded the most headroom, where the sloping roofs of the old colony building met. The skin on his hands, Petra noted, was gnarled, flecked with tiny white scars, the same as those Maratse had – the marks of a hunter, or someone who worked with sharp implements. But it was arthritis that twisted Korniliu's fingers, he explained, as he sat down. "The desk makes me feel strong, imagining the hunt at sea, the crash of the waves, the thump of ice against the hull. But these fingers," he said, lifting his hands. "Well, I struggle to write with them now. I dictate all my mails – in Danish, of course. It seems Greenlandic is one of the few languages to still baffle technology – no dictation software yet. Still." He smiled, revealing large gaps between tiny teeth. "I like the fact that there's something about our culture that can slow the inevitable creep of technology. Which brings us nicely back to you. How can I help you, Commissioner?"

"Masks," Petra said, deciding she liked the old Greenlander.

"What do you want to know?"

"Everything."

Korniliu's eyes sparkled in the dim light from the overhead lamps. He reached out to switch on a desk lamp, then tapped the desk as he turned one way and then the other to look at the bookshelves lining the walls.

"Holmstedt's book is a good start. A good introduction to masks for someone short on time." Korniliu turned his head to look at Petra, smiling when she caught his eye. "I might have been away, Commissioner, but I do keep in touch with current events. It's not only the past that intrigues me, and I will admit to being intrigued by your killer."

"*My* killer?"

"*Aap*," he said. "It is *your* city after all."

"I'm not sure about that," Petra said. "But tell me what intrigues you."

Korniliu leaned over the desk, drawing Petra and Tiiu closer as he lowered his voice to a conspiratorial whisper. "It's the blend of magic, myth, and madness."

"You think he's mad?"

"Aren't all killers?"

"Not necessarily," Tiiu said. She bit her lip, as if being caught talking out of turn, but Petra encouraged her with a nod of her head. "He's probably suffering from something. So, he might be mentally ill – mental health issues, perhaps. But that doesn't mean he's mad. *Anaana*, my mother, struggles with depression. She's ill, not mad."

"But your mother doesn't kill people, Tiiu," Petra said.

"Sometimes I think she'd like to kill my brother." Tiiu laughed, only to turn serious a second later. "But the killer is using a mask. Maybe he…" She looked at Petra and shrugged. "*If* it's a *he*, then maybe he is disfigured somehow, and he's using the mask to hide his face. The woman at the church said he was wearing a mask. That means he's using them for two purposes."

"And the purpose," Korniliu said, "if I may, is what makes this so fascinating. Of course, you're quite right to suppose he is hiding his face behind the mask, but he could use any mask for that purpose. Your killer has chosen a Greenlandic mask, and judging by what I have seen in the media…"

"Yes," Petra said and sighed, thinking of the photo someone had taken of the boy wearing the mask at the Christmas market. "We couldn't stop that being circulated."

"Of course not, but no matter." Korniliu pushed his chair back and stood up. He pressed his face close to the bookshelf on his right, running twisted fingers through his thin black hair, then gripped the spine of a large dusty book. He pulled it off the shelf and dropped it onto the desk with a thump. Korniliu took a letter opener and slid it inside the flap of the book to open it, before repeating the action to turn to the pages he was looking for. "Here," he said, tapping the text with the tip of the blunt blade. "This passage tells us how the shaman used the mask to enter the spirit world. The masks would be made to symbolise the shaman's helper spirits. The mask possesses great strength, and it can metamorphose – it has the power of change. So, the wearer of the mask is not just using it to summon spirits, even though he will be strengthened by those spirits, through the mask. Your killer," Korniliu said, looking up, "gains strength from the mask, so perhaps he is suffering, but not necessarily from something he is ashamed of. I don't think he is using the mask to hide, but to transform. A mask is a powerful tool. It will make him strong."

"He's killing people," Petra said. "Is that the purpose of a mask?"

"*Naamik*," Korniliu said. "And this is where he seems to have combined the purposes of the mask with that of the *tupilaq*." Korniliu used the knife to flick through several more pages until he found the next relevant passage. He turned the book towards Petra and Tiiu, tapping a series of three black and white plates showing grotesque figures with bulbous eyes, large mouths, and engorged penises. "You've seen these in the gift shops, of course. This is what the *tupilaq* has become. But before they were carved for the tourists, *tupilaq* were made by a shaman to cause harm to someone." Korniliu leaned back in his chair, and said, "For example, suppose I was jealous of a man who was about to marry the woman I wanted to marry. I might employ a shaman to make a *tupilaq* to pursue that man and hurt him, perhaps even kill him. The shaman would make a figure in the form of the man, for example, but he would use powerful elements, such as bones from a dead child, human hair, teeth, binding them to a wooden figure, wrapping them in furs, and charging them with his seed. Thus, he created a real *tupilaq* and sent it forth, perhaps dropping it into the sea when the victim climbed into his *qajaq*. If the magic was strong enough, then maybe the man would die at sea – a freak wave, or perhaps a polar bear attack. But if the victim's magic was stronger than that of the shaman, then the magic might rebound and the *tupilaq* would kill the man who commissioned it."

"And the mask?" Petra said. "It's not a *tupilaq*."

"It's not, but he is using it as a weapon, thus combining the two things. But…" Korniliu fell silent for a moment. He reached for the letter opener, tapping the blade against the ends of his twisted fingers. "The curious thing about your killer is how he is blending a third thing into the mask."

"Such as?"

"Technology, Commissioner. He has printed a reproduction of the mask. He is charging it with a chemical…"

"Chlorine," Petra said, frowning as she wondered how much Korniliu knew, and how.

"I told him," Tiiu whispered. "When I set up the meeting. It seemed relevant."

"And it is," Korniliu said. "But what is fascinating about it, is the way this man is inspired by the old ways of the shaman – old Greenland magic – and bringing it into the twenty-first century, by using modern technology to fabricate his masks. On the one hand, he must have studied the art, and the lore, but he has taken the next step and mass-produced the mask, just like so many things are mass-produced today."

"That impresses you?" Petra asked.

"I suppose it does. But, on the other hand, seeing how he uses the masks, then it worries me. Greatly."

"Why?"

"Masks take time to make, Commissioner. Even today, with woodcarving tools, hobby drills, and the like. It is a work of art. It requires patience and time. Whatever patience your killer had when making the original, it is gone now. He has made his template, and he can take shortcuts, printing more masks at the press of a button. It suggests, Commissioner, that the killer has run out of patience, or he is running out of time. Perhaps both. Either way…"

"It makes him dangerous," Petra said.

"*Aap*," Korniliu said. "Very."

Marlunngorneq

Tuesday, 15th December 2043

Chapter 15

The grey wall at the back of the prison chapel was decorated with an intricate snowflake. Natuk stared at it, following the artist's lines, searching for repetitive patterns, smiling when she found one, before searching for another. The chapel windows looked out onto the sea, where the white growlers of ice – now blue in the grey light beneath the snow clouds – surged like dodgems towards the beach. The concept for the prison, as far as Natuk understood, was to add a therapeutic dimension to incarceration. Not only was the prison the first of its kind in Greenland – finished in 2019, to provide a means of housing prisoners in a secure facility previously unavailable in the country – it was also experimental. For those inmates whose crimes were more trivial, but still required time behind bars, it was thought that windows looking out at the sea would allow them to nurture their connection with nature. They would be able to see life continue, and, perhaps, to desire to be a part of it once more. The interior design of the prison reflected the same therapeutic mission, displaying Inuit art on the walls, such as the snowflake in the chapel, the twists of northern lights on the walls of the sports hall, and even the occasional sealskin and polar bear skin draped over this chair, that bench. Natuk wondered, however, if the sight of fishing trawlers plying the seas outside an inmate's window, might not have the opposite effect, reminding them of what they were missing, teasing them with the sight of something they longed for but could not have. Natuk knew it would probably drive her nuts, which was why she preferred solitary, and the windowless cells of the maximum-security facility in the centre of the prison. Of course, the occasional trip to the chapel was *nice*, and so long as the prison staff thought her soul could be saved, Natuk decided to play along.

The interview, however, surprised her.

She had heard snatches of Kaapi Samøssen's show through the year, but never an entire programme. It amused her that he wanted to interview her, and even more so that he had been given permission to do so. *Perhaps*, she thought, *I'm no longer public enemy number one.* Losing the top slot might have annoyed her for a moment, if it hadn't been for the rewards that came along with the interview, such as the visit to the chapel – cuffs off, according to the Lutheran pastor's orders – and a prolonged shower. It seemed that Kaapi Samøssen had some sway with prison management, and the least they could do was show their prize prisoner at her best.

"Time, Natuk," the guard said.

She turned on the bench, then held out her wrists for the cuffs, then her feet for the ankle bracelets. She might have showered, dressed in a clean prison suit, but management wanted to show off their hardware too, completing the image of a hardened prisoner.

Kaapi Samøssen, by comparison, was positively scruffy.

His haphazard mix of jeans with sealskin *kamiks* on his feet, the tie-dyed 60s throwback t-shirt and the strong polar bear amulet he wore around his neck, gave Natuk pause, as she wondered if this was the man management wanted to impress, and why.

"It's all about the ratings," Kaapi said, as he reached out to shake Natuk's hand. The guard hissed and he pulled back his hand, returning Natuk's lopsided smile with an awkward one of his own. "Like I was saying, it's about ratings. You're going to boost them and boost the prison's profile at the same time."

"And that's why they let you in?"

"*Imaqa*, maybe. But maybe it's because I'm banging the First Minister, eh?"

Natuk frowned as they sat down. "That's not how you talk on the radio," she said.

"You're a fan?"

"I'm not a *fan*. But I've heard your show every now and again."

"Radio," Kaapi said, "is, and has always been, important in Greenland. This is an important time in our lives – independence. So, we go back to our roots. Embrace our past and use it to build our future. Sure, there's all kinds of technologies, and we're streaming this and streaming that, but voice… The human voice." Kaapi smiled, and Natuk recognised the man she had heard on the radio, now that he had switched out his bravado with passion.

"It's so intimate. It's me and it's you. You hear my voice, and I'm talking to *you*. Put a pair of cans on."

"Cans?"

"Headphones." Kaapi pointed to his satchel and pulled out a pair of headphones Natuk imagined a DJ might wear. "Good ones will put my voice right into your head. Which is why," he said, tossing the headphones back inside the satchel, "this will not be live."

"It's not?"

"No." Kaapi glanced at the guard before continuing. "They're worried about your voice getting into people's heads."

"I'm in prison."

"For good reason, I understand." Kaapi grinned. "No offence."

"If I was offended, you'd be dead."

Kaapi's response died on his lips as Natuk fixed him with a neutral stare.

"You're kidding," he said.

"Offend me and find out." Natuk licked her top lip as Kaapi turned to look at the guard. "He's too far away," she said, lowering her voice to a whisper. "I mean, if you think I can't…"

"No," Kaapi said, recovering. "We're good. I believe you. I just wish I'd recorded that bit." He took a long breath, ran his hand through his thick black hair, then reached into his satchel. "I have a mic for you. It clips onto your collar," he said, reaching forward. "If I may?"

"You're very polite, all of a sudden," Natuk said, lifting her chin.

"You said you could kill me if I offended you."

"I did."

Kaapi laughed. "So, I changed tack."

"Very wise." Natuk lowered her head once Kaapi had clipped the mic to her collar. She caught a flicker of something in his eye – a reflection of the light, or a flash of inspiration. It didn't matter. Whatever it was, she decided it suited him, adding to his crazy look.

"We're just going to get right to it then," Kaapi said, as he set up the recorder, slipped his cans over his head, and adjusted his own mic. "Whenever you're ready, I'll start asking questions."

"No introduction?"

"I'll do that in post." He checked his watch. "I've only got half an hour."

"Fine," Natuk said. "Ask away."

Kaapi did a silent count from five on his fingers, then launched straight in. "Tell me about masks," he said.

"Masks?"

"Greenland masks. You used one as a symbol on your propaganda, and you printed many more."

"It wasn't propaganda," Natuk said, stiffening a little as Kaapi fiddled with the input and output levels. He waved his hand for her to keep talking. "I needed an image people could identify with."

"And could they?"

"I think every Greenlander knows what a mask looks like."

"And if they didn't," Kaapi said. "They do now. So, Natuk Petersen, what if I said you were the inspiration for the killer stalking the streets of Nuuk. What would you say to that?"

"That you were wrong. That you were…"

"Stupid?" He cut her off. "Maybe it is a long shot, but you tried to turn the people of Nuuk against the government. You used a mask as a symbol. You showed him how effective it can be. One could also say you inspired him to print the copies he's leaving on his victims. What do you think this masked killer is trying to say?"

"You think I inspired him?"

"*Aap*. I do."

"I used my masks for a specific purpose. I respected our cultural history. I didn't abuse that symbol." Natuk snorted. "You think he has an agenda?"

"He might."

"I doubt it. If he has, he's blown it. He's leaving his masks at the scene of the crime. They're not symbols, they're murder weapons, like a cloth soaked in chloroform. There's no symbology in it."

"He's printed masks inspired by Greenlandic masks worn by shaman. He's digging into our past, bringing it into our future."

"He's twisting our past." Natuk shook her head at the thought of it. She looked at Kaapi, and said, "Masks were powerful items. They were destroyed after use. You didn't leave them lying around. That's disrespect. It's also dangerous. That power could be used against you. This killer…" Natuk laughed. "This coward doesn't understand what he's got. And he's taken something, whatever the inspiration, and he's made cheap plastic copies. He probably stole a mask from a private collection, then ran it through a 3D scanner."

"You don't think he made it himself? The original?"

"I don't know if he did, but if he was going to do this right, he would spend time on each mask, not grab one from the top of a stack. Besides," she said, warming to the subject. "He's using them wrong."

"How?"

"He's weaponised something, the original purpose of which was to gain access to the spirit world, not to kill with."

"You used a mask."

"I used the *image* of a mask. There's a difference." Natuk thought back to when she had surprised Tiina Markussen, the young woman she had reinvented as *Viola*, with a mask on *Mitaartut*. *That was different,* she thought. *That was traditional. It was respectful.*

"Natuk?"

"What?"

"It seemed like you were deep in thought. Is there something about this killer that you can identify with?"

"In what way?" Natuk tilted her head to one side, and added, "Remember, you don't want to offend me, Kaapi."

The way he smiled back at her, Natuk wondered if, actually, he did.

"You ran a campaign of terror on the streets of Nuuk."

"I had a political agenda."

"It doesn't matter." Kaapi shrugged, goading her. "You scared people."

"I told them the truth."

"You used people – a young woman. She died for your truth."

"People die," Natuk said. Her chains rattled as she squirmed in her seat. "All the time. They die for things they love, things they believe in."

"And you believed in your cause, to keep Greenland in the clutches of its colonial masters?"

"I believed in what was best for Greenland."

"Was?"

"*Is*."

"And you still believe that Greenland would be better off in the hands of the Danes?"

"That," Natuk said, pausing for breath, "is what I believed." Another pause. "What I believed then."

"And now?"

Natuk laughed. "I'm reformed."

"Really? You've seen the error of your ways?"

"*Aap*."

"And you would denounce your actions?"

"I would."

"So, the tiger has been tamed."

"What?"

"You have been castrated."

"Kaapi," Natuk said, leaning forward. "I'm a woman."

"Castrated," he said.

Natuk saw the smile play across Kaapi's lips. She considered how much force she would have to apply when wrapping the chain between her wrists around his neck. It was a short chain, but if she pulled him off his chair, onto the ground, stuffed her knees into her back, she might just kill him before the guard pulled her off. But beyond the instant gratification of causing him pain, she saw an opportunity. Had he not said something about putting her voice into people's heads? Something about intimacy.

"Yes," Natuk said, thinking it through, seeing the opportunity he had given her.

"Care to expand upon that?"

Natuk took a quick breath, and said, "I made a mistake. I was angry. My brother was dead. My adoptive mother had twisted us both. We were casualties of a war of her making."

"You were soldiers."

"*Aap*."

"And you went to war."

"For the wrong side. I see that now."

"And that's what you would tell the people of Nuuk?"

"The people of Greenland," Natuk said. "I'd tell them I was sorry, if I had the chance."

"I'm giving it you," Kaapi said. "Right now. This is it."

"Then I am sorry." Natuk settled in her chair, chains rattling as she stretched her feet to the limit of her tethers. "I'm sorry for what I did."

"And what about him? The killer? Any words for him?"

"None."

"You've got nothing to say to him?"

"Maybe if we met one day." Natuk lifted her chin to indicate the room and the prison. "If they catch him, if they don't kill him, he'll end up here."

"And do you think they'll catch him?"

"If he keeps leaving his masks behind, they will. That's powerful magic. In the wrong hands, it could be used against him. He's being careless. If he keeps that up, they'll catch him."

"You're sure about that?"

"*Aap*," she said. "Definitely."

Pingasunngorneq

Wednesday, 16th December 2043

Chapter 16

Josef buried the mask forty-eight hours earlier, after which, powerless, he drifted through the streets of Nuuk, turned by the wind, weighed down by the snow, and chilled through to the marrow. He couldn't speak when the woman found him, had barely the strength to take her arm as she pulled him out of the snow, onto his feet, one arm tucked around his waist as she walked him to the nearest café. She settled him on a seat, took a step towards the counter, then paused, taking his shoulder, pushing him towards the wall until his head rested against it.

"I'm going to get you something to drink and something to eat," she said.

He slid down in his seat until the metal edge of the round table pinched his head against the wall. She lifted his head, gently, when she returned, saying something about *ten minutes until the food arrives* and then *it's warm in here. Let me help you out of your jacket.*

She said nothing about the smell as she opened his jacket, and the look on her face suggested it wasn't the first time she had helped someone off the street.

"I just hoped it wouldn't be you, Josef," she said, pulling his hood back, and, finally, getting a response.

He opened his eyes.

"There you are."

The food came. She helped him eat it. Tugging the white cotton gloves from his fingers, tucking them into his pockets, and then working his hands like a stop-motion puppeteer – pressing finger and thumb together, moving back, then helping again, tiny movements guiding the fork in his hand to the sausage on his plate, to his mouth.

"You're in a terrible state," she said.

He chewed. Slowly. She guided his hand, plucking the fork from his hand once he had a mouthful to cut the rest of the sausage. She cut the bigger fries in half.

"Never mind them," she said, when a group of students sniggered. "They don't know what you've been through.

She helped him finish the plate, then slipped a paper straw into his soda, pressing the end between his lips, holding it there as he drank.

"I remember one of the last times I saw you," she said, repositioning his straw. "It was a bad day, like this one. But you were so young. It was when those boys forced you to pee on the bleach block in the urinal. You were so small you couldn't reach. They held you up by your arms. You won't remember the details, but that's what they told us, once we caught them. You were so close to the bleach that when you peed on it the fumes knocked you out." She smiled, patted his hand. "It happens more often than you think. But the boys said you drooled, and they let go of you. That's when you hit your head, Josef. But you won't remember. It's the reason you forget things. Even now. Just looking at you. I can see you forget things."

"I try to remember."

"I know you do. But it's not your fault. You were just a small boy with no one to stand up for you. You're a man now, Josef. The last I heard you had a job."

"*Aap*."

"Do you still have it?"

"I don't remember. I think I called in sick."

"Do you get sick often?"

He looked up, blinking as he tried to focus. There was something familiar about the woman, and the things she knew – so many things he had forgotten.

"You don't remember who I am. Do you?"

"I can't…"

"It's okay," she said. "My name is Makkak Lind. I was the school counsellor. We met every month. Sometimes more often than that. I got to know your parents too. I came to your father's funeral. But…" Makkak's smile faded. She reached out for Josef's hand. "I retired before you left school. I'm sorry about that, Josef. I really am."

"You left Nuuk."

"For a little while. That's right."

"When *anaana* died…"

"They put you in the children's home. I know. A friend told me. She also told me you made lots of progress."

"They helped me remember."

"Yes, they did." The smile on Makkak's face

flattened, and she squeezed his hand once more, reaching out with her other hand to smooth her wrinkled fingers over his knuckles. "They told me it was difficult for you to remember the good things…"

"There are no good things."

"Well, that's not quite right, but bad things are sometimes easier to remember."

"I had a list," he said.

"I know about the list." Makkak pulled her hands back and clasped them in her lap. "I must confess, they told me more than they should, Josef. I was retired, you know. But I always felt a little sorry for you."

"I made a list of nine things," he said, carrying on as if he hadn't heard her. "I don't remember the order, but I remember being chased. I remember the Danish man – the teacher. He let them hurt me."

"I remember him," Makkak said. "He left Nuuk at the end of your fourth year in school."

"You were my counsellor," he said, looking up.

"We met once a month."

"You left me."

"I retired, Josef."

"And another one came, someone who said they would help me."

"Yes."

"They didn't."

"I'm sure they tried. It wasn't an easy time for you. I'm sure they did everything they could."

"*Anaana* died."

"Yes, but Josef, no one could stop that. She took her own life."

"Then I was alone."

"That's not right. You had help. Your life got better."

"How do you know that?"

Makkak lowered her voice as Josef raised his.

"I told you… I had a friend." She changed topics. "They said you developed an interest in Greenland's history, that you read lots and lots of books."

It hit him then, the heat of the café, the weight of his parka, hanging loosely from his shoulders.

The mask.

He doubled up in the chair, as if a great stone turned inside his stomach.

"Josef?"

It could have been the heat, after two days and nights wandering alone in the cold. But he knew it was the power of the mask rebounding, hitting him full force, slamming invisible fists into his stomach, forcing the contents up and out of his mouth as he vomited onto the table. Makkak gasped, turning her head as Josef emptied his stomach. The students were silent, watching. Josef raised his head, wiped his mouth with the back of his hand, and then turned. He ran out of the café, shoving at the door as the bottom lip caught on the ice glued to the grille on the top step. He stumbled into the street, then straightened as the cool air cleared his head. He saw a bus approaching a stop, read the sign, and ran towards it, fumbling his bus card from the pocket of his parka, then pressing it against the screen beside the driver before flopping into the first vacant seat.

The bus pulled away from the stop, and Josef closed his eyes.

The teenagers between the first and second floor of his apartment block grinned as he shuffled up the stairs. They flicked their cigarettes at him, laughing when the ends sparked off his parka.

"Where've you been?" they asked.

Josef kept walking, turning on the landing to climb to the next floor. He stopped outside his apartment door, turned the handle, and then again, harder.

"It's locked, you idiot," the teenagers said.

Josef remembered what he had forgotten. He had no key.

"I can't get in," he said, as one of the teens followed him up the stairs.

"Climb in through your kitchen window," the boy said. "It's open."

"I'm too tired." Josef pressed his hand against the door, felt the wind stiffen the hairs on his skin. Somehow, he had survived two more nights on the streets, but now, he realised, he was going to die outside his apartment.

The power of the mask had rebounded.

"I can climb in," the boy said.

Josef turned his head towards the boy, then nodded.

"Hey," the boy said, calling to the teenagers on the landing below. "I'm going to climb into his apartment."

"You're going to break in?"

"*Naamik*, I'm going to climb in. He said I

could."

Josef felt the vibration of the teenagers' steps as they climbed the stairs, pushing past him to help their friend through the window. They gave him a leg up, then pushed at his heels, grinning at the sound of pots and pans crashing to the floor inside the kitchen. The boy stuck his face through the window, then his arm, grabbing for one of the other teenagers' hands, pulling them up as the others pushed. Josef watched as the kitchen window swallowed one teenager after the other, until he was alone outside his apartment.

The crashing inside continued, together with shouts of *you can't piss there*, followed by *just watch me*. Josef rested his head against the door, too tired and too cold to move. When they finally opened it, he fell into the tiny hallway which is where they left him, stepping over his body as the wind blew in from the sea, dusting Josef and the hallway with new snow.

Josef felt something clawing at his ankle – a bony hand. Perhaps it was one of the helper spirits. Âmo had long arms with bony hands. The shaman used Âmo as protection, placing him in front of a special place, or a house, or a thing. Âmo would grip the ankles of intruders and thieves, invisible hands wrapped around their ankles, slowing them down if they tried to run away, holding them steady if they tried to attack. Josef couldn't remember calling Âmo. This was different.

"Hey."

The spirit had a voice.

"You need to wake up."

Josef grimaced as he turned his head. He opened one eye, then the other, blinking in the light outside his apartment, until the boy's face gained shape, and he recognised him as the first of the teenagers to climb through the window.

"I'm sorry about what they did. But the door's open now. You should go in."

Josef rolled onto his side. He felt the boy push at his heels, pushing him further along the hallway, into his apartment.

"You really should get up."

Josef blinked again. He rubbed his face, twisting the base of his hand into his eyes. He looked at the boy and then stared at the boy's teeth.

"What?" the boy said.

"I need your help."

"I've already helped you." The boy pointed at the kitchen, then at Josef's feet. "I opened the door. Now I got you inside."

"One more thing."

"I don't know."

"I need something from downstairs."

"You haven't got a downstairs."

"The basement," Josef said.

"I'm not carrying you to the basement."

"I can walk."

Josef held out his hand, and the boy pulled him to his feet, wrinkling his nose as Josef zipped his parka.

"You smell like a drunk."

"I'm not."

"*Imaqa*, but you smell like one."

Josef reached past the boy and checked that the lock on the door was fixed in the open position. He bent down as if to tie his shoelace, removing the key to the basement from the space under the floorboard. He nodded at the stairs and they left the apartment. Josef pulled the door closed behind him, then opened it.

"Just checking," he said.

The boy led the way, calling over his shoulder to Josef as he followed. "What's in the basement."

"Something I need."

"Is it heavy?"

"*Naamik.*"

"Then why can't you get it?"

"I need help. You said you would help me."

"*Aap*," the boy said with a shrug. He stopped as they reached the ground floor. "It wasn't me that pissed in your bed. Just so you know."

"It doesn't matter," Josef said, as he unlocked the basement door. "You're helping me."

"Yeah, okay," the boy said. He smiled at Josef, revealing a full set of brilliant white teeth.

Sisamanngorneq

Thursday, 17th December 2043

Chapter 17

The chairs in the waiting area of the First Minister's outer office were draped with sealskins. The wooden legs were salvaged from *qajaq* frames from the north, according to the plaque screwed into the wall beside the chairs. Another *qajaq* frame was suspended from the high ceiling. Petra squinted at the lights shining through the frame, and at the perfect shadow cast onto the opposite wall above the door to Pipaluk Uutaaq's office. The *qajaq* made her think of Maratse. She turned to look at Danielsen sitting beside her and decided to tell him about the video.

"I *have* been distracted," she said.

"Since the funeral. I know."

"Yes, the funeral, but lately too." Petra turned in her seat, gesturing at Pipaluk's door. "This is for show, you have to understand that. It's important for her to put on a show, but whatever she says when we're inside, you can trust that she means it, and that she will do what she says, however irrational it may be. She has that power now. We have to get used to it. Which is why," she said, drawing a breath, "I want you to know that I am not fully committed to the job. I haven't been for a while."

"I don't know," Danielsen said.

"Yes, Aqqa, you do know. You've known for a long time. I think we can drop all the pretence now. You heard a rumour that I almost quit, and I did – I wrote my letter of resignation, and Aron Ulloriaq was about to file it. But then Natuk happened, and I was consumed by it all. But now, there's something else, another reason I'm ready to step down." Petra pulled her phone out of her pocket and turned the screen towards Danielsen. "It's a video of David. There's no sound."

Danielsen watched in silence, and then said, "Who sent it to you?"

"I don't know. The sender masked their address. Masked." Petra let a soft laugh pass between her lips. "It's appropriate, don't you think?"

"It's not related."

"I don't believe so. But the timing is interesting. A year after his funeral, and someone sends me a video."

"Who is he hugging?"

"I don't know."

Danielsen leaned back in his chair. He tapped his fingers on his knee, and said, "Maratse didn't hug."

"I know." Petra slipped her phone into her pocket. "It's driving me mad. And I have no answers. I asked Natuk…"

"You think she sent you the video?"

"No." Petra frowned, as if the thought had never occurred to her. "How could she?"

Danielsen started to speak, then stopped as Iista said the First Minister was ready for them. "Don't tell Pipaluk about the video," he said, as he stood up.

"Agreed. But promise me one thing." Petra straightened her jacket as she stood up. "Let me take the fall in there. No," she said, pressing her hand on Danielsen's arm as he protested. "She might be mad at you, but she's always mad at me. She remembers when I investigated her father."

"For the murder of Tinka Winther."

"It's a long time ago. I think she was thirteen. But she hasn't forgotten." Petra pointed at the door. "Shall we?"

Pipaluk waited until they were both seated and then picked up a remote from her desk. "I want to play you something," she said, pointing the remote at a multimedia panel set into the wall.

"He's twisting our past." Natuk Petersen's voice burst into the room the second Pipaluk pressed the button. *"Masks were powerful items. They were destroyed after use. You didn't leave them lying around. That's disrespect. It's also dangerous. That power could be used against you. This killer... This coward doesn't understand what he's got. And he's taken something, whatever the inspiration, and he's made cheap plastic copies. He probably stole a mask from a private collection, then ran it through a 3D scanner."*

"That," Pipaluk said, pressing pause on the remote, "is more information than I have received from either of you. Can you tell me why an ex-police officer, currently incarcerated in the most secure part of Nuuk Prison, has a better grip on this so-called *masked killer* than you do?"

"First Minister…" Danielsen said, before Petra interrupted.

"Natuk Petersen has an exceptionally methodical mind, First Minister," Petra said.

"As she demonstrated in January."

"Yes. She is a talented officer."

"A prisoner, Petra. There is a difference. She no longer works for you. And yet, her insight was refreshing, albeit potentially damaging. I used to think Kaapi Samøssen understood his role in the new, independent Greenland. I think we will have to review his position and his relationship to this government. I can't have irresponsible broadcasts with the potential to incite further violence, perhaps even death, especially when the Commissioner and…" She looked at Danielsen. "Her potential replacement, are proving wholly inept at catching this murderer." She held up her hand, stopping Petra from speaking. "I've had the Chinese and the Dutch on the phone every day this week. They want assurances that this isn't another *Calendar Man* episode, and that we will contain this murderous spree within our city limits. I reminded them, of course, that they were guests in Greenland, and that our city limits stretched across the length and breadth of the entire country. But if this situation isn't contained, then perhaps I will be tempted to review their offers of assistance."

"We have received an offer of help from the Americans," Danielsen said.

"Perfect. And how is that going to look? Americans, and our migrant neighbours, combining forces to locate and stop a single madman running free in our city?"

"You're worried about how this looks," Petra said. "I understand."

"I'm worried about how this *ends*, Commissioner. The world is watching. Greenland is an emerging country, admittedly with a long, rich history of culture and tradition, but now that culture is being thrown back in our faces. If it isn't enough that Kaapi Samøssen made a link to Natuk Petersen's terror campaign on his show, *she* then goaded this killer, after which she apologised to the people of Nuuk and Greenland for her previous actions." Pipaluk tossed the remote onto her desk. "My office will take care of Kaapi. But I want to know what the two of you are doing to take care of *him*."

"You mean the suspect?"

"Yes, Commissioner. That's exactly who I mean. Who else?"

Petra stood up to leave.

"Didn't I just ask you to tell me what you're doing about it?"

"You did," Petra said. "And we are processing the scenes, collating evidence, doubling patrols in the city."

"But no curfew, Commissioner. You're still letting people onto the streets."

"We're talking about one suspect. Not a citywide riot, First Minister."

"But if you shut the city down, and then went door to door, or whatever it is you do…"

"We would create a panic," Danielsen said. He

stood up.

"There is already a *panic*, Inspector. People are being murdered. Christmas – the nation's first truly independent Christmas after the referendum – is seven days away. The media is full of speculation. People are asking questions. They even interviewed a young man who the Commissioner chased into the sea."

"Miilu Bendtsen," Petra said. "We let him off with a warning."

"And is that supposed to make me feel safe?" Pipaluk slid her fingers into her hair, clenching them in a fist. "You need to make this a priority."

"It is a priority, First Minister."

"Then tell the people, Commissioner. I shouldn't have to be the one to hold a press conference to explain what the police is or isn't doing to make the city safe again." She let go of her hair and slapped her hand on the desk. "Do your jobs. Find the killer. Save Christmas. It's that simple. Or, if you can't," Pipaluk gestured at the speakers on the wall. "I'll find someone who can."

"Natuk Petersen?" Danielsen laughed, and then, "You're serious?"

"Of course, I'm not serious." Pipaluk snorted. "But now that she's apologised, who knows what I might do. At least *she's* keeping me informed."

Petra tapped Danielsen's arm and pointed at the door. Pipaluk dismissed them with a wave, calling for Iista to set up a call with the radio station as soon as Petra opened the door. Danielsen led the way to the elevator, saying nothing until they were both inside and the doors were closed.

"We could do a press conference."

"And what would we tell people?" Petra said as she pressed the button for the ground floor. "We have nothing to go on. There has been one sighting of a potential suspect. Each of the crime scenes has been clean – no DNA other than the victim's. There's nothing linking the victims…"

"Nothing that we've found," Danielsen said.

"And the only break we had led to a minor bust for possession of hash, and a head cold." Petra shook her head at the absurdity of it all, and to clear her mind of the lingering image she had of Commander Joshua Seabloom on her couch. "I'm really not cut out for this anymore," she whispered.

"What?"

"Nothing."

The doors opened as the lift settled on the ground floor. Petra stepped out of the elevator and walked straight into Constable Tiiu Mikkiki.

"There's been a development," Tiiu said, once she had apologised for startling Petra.

"Keep talking, Constable," Danielsen said.

"It's best if you come with me."

Tiiu turned and walked at a brisk pace to the main entrance. She led the way across the parking lot separating the government building from the police station. Tiiu opened the door and ushered them inside, pointing to the left and directing them to the first of two interview rooms.

"Her name is Makkak Lind," she said, as she stopped outside the door. "She used to be a school counsellor. She's retired, and she's concerned about one of her ex-pupils." Tiiu beamed as she said the name, “Josef Filemonsen.”

“Okay. How is this related?” Petra said.

Tiiu held out her hand. “Wait. There’s more.” She pulled out her phone and swiped the screen to open her notes. “We also had a call from Nuuk Import. They supply most of the companies and institutions in Greenland, via their warehouses in Nuuk. When Inspector Danielsen briefed us to track down sources of chlorine in the city, we focused on the obvious. It took a few more days before someone contacted Nuuk Import.” Tiiu’s eyes widened as she reached the end of her notes. “They checked their supplies, and they are missing a four-litre bottle of chlorine.”

“From their stores?”

“*Aap*. But they said they wouldn’t have thought much about it, if they weren’t missing one of their staff, also.”

Danielsen gestured at the door. “Josef…”

“Filemonsen,” Tiiu said.

“I need an address,” Danielsen said.

Tiiu handed him her phone, highlighting her notes with a swipe of her finger and thumb.

“Tiiu and I will take the interview,” Petra said.

“I’ll assemble a team.” Danielsen slapped Tiiu’s phone into her hand. “Good work, Constable.”

“I’m just the messenger,” she said. “But thanks.”

Danielsen left them outside the interview room. Petra watched him go, then looked at Tiiu, laughing at the smile on the young Constable’s face.

“You did well, Tiiu.”

"*Qujanaq*."

Petra peered in through the tiny glass window in the door. "Have you talked to her?"

"Only a little. I said I would find some coffee. But I came looking for you first."

"Okay. Find that coffee, then come in and join us. Oh, and one more thing," Petra said, as Tiiu turned to leave.

"Ma'am?"

"Set up another meeting with Natuk Petersen."

"Why?"

"It's a hunch, but I have an idea she might be useful before the end."

"You want to bring her outside the prison?"

"I haven't got that far yet. Just set up a meeting, or a visit – whatever we call it. And see if Korniliu can join us."

"Ma'am, aren't we going to arrest Josef Filemonsen?"

"That's the plan."

"Then why…"

"Because sometimes plans fail, Tiiu. And we can't afford more mistakes." Petra tapped Tiiu's phone and said, "Make the calls. Bring coffee."

She watched Tiiu walk away. She took a breath, straightened her hair, and then knocked on the door before opening it.

"Makkak Lind," she said. "My name is Commissioner Jensen. You wanted to talk about Josef?"

Tallimanngorneq

Friday, 18th December 2043

Chapter 18

There was a time, before he moved to Nuuk, when Inspector Danielsen was very impressed with the men and women of the police Special Response Unit, much to the chagrin of Uummannaq Chief of Police Torben Simonsen. The calendar was full of training and Danielsen remembered badgering Simonsen to let him go, to try out for the SRU. Sergeant Gaba Alatak, the SRU leader at the time, had put a stopper in Danielsen's ambitions, encouraging him to try harder next time. And then, many years later, Danielsen was himself at the front of a team breaking down doors with an arrest order for a killer – twice in the same month. He might have found some irony in the situation, if he had time to chew it over. Instead, he clicked the mic twice to signal to the SRU team waiting on the stairwell below that he was ready to enter.

"Ready?" he said to the officers on both sides of the door. When they nodded, he knocked, holding his breath as he waited for a response.

After half a minute, Danielsen knocked again. After the third knock he checked the address, and then stepped back, waving the officer with the breaching tool forwards. He had heard some of his colleagues call the sixteen-kilogramme steel tool a universal key, which made sense to anyone who had seen it in action. But when the young constable stepped forward to swing the tool into the door, Danielsen worried what they might find on the other side.

The door splintered and the officers on either side of the door entered, guns drawn, yelling *Police! Police!* Danielsen waited for the officer with the breaching tool to drop it, and then tapped him on the shoulder, following him into the apartment.

As soon as the officers cleared the apartment, checking each room and pronouncing it empty, Danielsen fiddled with the camera mounted to his bulletproof vest, and then slipped an earbud into his ear.

"Commissioner," he said. "Are you getting this?"

"Yes."

Danielsen increased the volume to hear Petra's voice over the sound of the team searching the apartment. He talked her through each room, skipping to the important details.

"Books about masks and a dictionary on the desk. Some tools." He brushed the books to one side and pointed at a small gouger. "Could have been used on the original mask."

"Inspector," one of the constables said, calling from the kitchen.

Danielsen followed the sound of his men into the kitchen, adjusting the camera so Petra could see what one of them was holding.

"Looks like chlorine," he said. "We'll get a serial number and see if it matches the one missing from Nuuk Import. There's a tin of paint too."

Danielsen stepped closer to the kitchen table, zooming in with the camera. "Boat paint."

"What about the rest of the apartment?" Petra asked.

"Nothing much. It's messy. Like the kitchen." Danielsen walked across the hall into the bedroom. "Smells of urine in here."

He checked the bathroom.

"The toothbrush is dry. So is the sink and shower. He might not have been home for a few days."

"That fits with what Makkak Lind, the school counsellor said. When she found him, she said it looked like he had been on the street for a few days. I've sent Tiiu to the children's home to see what she can dig up."

Danielsen thought about what he knew of Petra Jensen – something about her being an orphan, and a resident of the same children's home.

"There's nothing here," he said, focusing again on the apartment. "I'll have some of the constables document everything, once the tech team has been in to pull biometrics." Danielsen paused as the SRU team cut into the communication channel. "Wait a minute, Commissioner. Stay on the line."

Danielsen walked out of the apartment to meet one of the SRU men standing at the top of the stairs.

"We've got a teenager downstairs," the officer said. "He says he and his friends were inside the apartment a couple of days ago."

"He knows Josef Filemonsen?"

"Not by name. But he and his mates crawled in through the kitchen window. It seems that

Filemonsen forgot his key. His apartment was locked, and the boys opened it for him." The officer adjusted the sling of his MP5 as he talked. "He also suggested they might have been a bit naughty."

"Naughty?"

"It's not the word he used. He said they pranked Filemonsen – pissed in his bed and generally messed things up."

"Smart."

"They don't know much about him."

"Did he see any masks?"

"No, but he says one of his friends is missing. A boy called Lukka Miiungi. Lukka was the first to climb in through the window. Turns out that he felt a bit bad about what they did. He said he wanted to go back and apologise. The kid down there…" The officer pointed. "Said no one wanted to go, but that he hasn't seen Lukka since."

"And Lukka visited Josef Filemonsen alone?"

"As far as I know."

"Okay, I'll come down." Danielsen took one step and then stopped as his phone rang. "Danielsen," he said, answering the call. He listened as the officer on the other end of the line gave him the latest information on the two old men: Luutivik Dalgaard and Sauli Mathiasen. Danielsen had experienced it before, after a drought of information, suddenly everything arrived at once. "Say that again," he said, waiting, then clicking his fingers for the SRU man to come closer as he ended the call. "The two men we found at the end of November – they were amateur craftsmen. Apparently, there's a basement in this block. It's a workshop."

"This block?"

"*Aap*."

"We'll secure it."

Danielsen stepped to one side, letting the SRU officer pass, and then called for one of the constables from the apartment to join him.

"Aqqa?" Petra's voice crackled into his ear. "What's going on?"

"Just a minute, Commissioner." Danielsen turned to the constable, then pointed at the teenager at the bottom of the stairs. "Look after him, get a statement. Then stay with him."

"Right, Inspector."

Danielsen followed the constable down the stairs, clicking his mic to talk to Petra as he moved from one floor to the next.

"There's a workshop in the basement of the building. The two old men who died on the first Advent Sunday used it. We found tools in Josef Filemonsen's apartment. It makes sense that he used it too. Maybe," Danielsen said, as the thought occurred to him, "he killed the two old men to cover his tracks."

"Or to try out his method," Petra said.

"Right."

Danielsen jogged around the side of the building to where the SRU team were stacked up either side of the basement door, ready to force entry.

"Aqqa," Petra said, as Danielsen reached the SRU team.

"*Aap*?"

"If he killed the two old men, then he was hiding something in the basement. You might want to prepare the team for what they might find."

"Will do," Danielsen said, only to realise he was too late as the SRU team used a breaching charge on the lock and kicked the door open. He held his breath as they tossed a flashbang grenade into the basement. The SRU team burst into the room a second after the grenade went off, clearing the room in less time than it had taken Danielsen's team to break down the door to Josef's apartment. Danielsen felt the surge of adrenaline in his blood as he thought back to his more impressionable days as a young constable. But the adrenaline faded as soon as the SRU leader stepped out of the basement and waved him over.

"We found a body," the officer said.

"Josef Filemonsen?"

"*Naamik.*" The SRU officer glanced over at the teenager, giving his statement to one of Danielsen's constables. "It's a teenage boy. I'm guessing it's Lukka Miiungi." The man grabbed Danielsen's arm as he took a step towards the basement. "It's not pretty, Inspector."

Danielsen nodded. He entered the basement with the SRU officer right behind him.

"I need to see, Aqqa," Petra said in his ear. "Don't even think about covering the camera."

"No, ma'am," he said. "I won't."

Danielsen followed the SRU men's directions, slowing as he spotted the boy's bare feet, and the pool of blood around his ankles. He took a step closer, careful to stay clear of the body, but close enough to look at the boy's face.

"I need more light," Petra said. "For the camera."

Danielsen took the flashlight from his belt and clicked it on. He shone it on the boy's face, tightening the spot of light on the boy's mouth, noting the missing front teeth, top and bottom. He drifted the light down the boy's face to his neck, swallowing as he spotted the tool in the side of the boy's throat.

"What is that, Aqqa?" Petra asked.

"It looks like a carving tool. Like the one I found in the apartment."

"And his teeth?"

Danielsen moved the light back to the boy's mouth. He let the camera linger there, heard Petra's gasp, and then took a step back.

"There's no one else in here?" he asked the SRU team.

"Just the boy," the leader said. "Although, you might find this interesting."

Danielsen followed the SRU officer to the other end of the basement, frowning as he took a step closer to something with blue lights glowing beneath a dustsheet.

"It's a 3D printer," the officer said. He pointed at the side of the machine and Danielsen lit it with his flashlight. "Property of Nuuk University, although I'm guessing it was donated."

"Strange thing to donate," Danielsen said. "Maybe it was thrown out?"

"*Imaqa*."

The SRU officer stepped away, then leaped to

the door as a face appeared in the doorway. Danielsen turned to see the SRU officer grab the teenage witness in a gentle but firm hug, carrying him out of the basement and away from the door before he could see anything. The sudden cry and wail from outside told Danielsen that the boy had seen more than he needed to.

"Aqqa," Petra said.

"Ma'am?"

"How many is it now?"

"That's five," he said.

"And the masks?"

"None yet. But…" Danielsen turned to look at the dead teenager. "He's changed his method. He stuck the tool in the boy's throat."

"And he took his teeth, that's important, Aqqa."

"Why?"

"It means he's not finished with the masks. He's trying to make them more powerful."

"By sticking a boy's teeth in them? That doesn't make any sense."

"Not to us. But if you look at the books in his apartment, I think you'll find it makes perfect sense."

Danielsen sighed, then pressed the mic close to his lips. "I'm going to need a minute."

"I understand. Take a minute, then set up the search. Don't worry about the budget. Get everyone you need, inside and outside the department. I'll brief the First Minister and I'll see you when you get back."

Danielsen turned off the chest camera and waved the SRU team over.

"We need to set up a search spiralling out from the basement."

"We'll need a lot of officers."

"You'll have them," Danielsen said. "I'll call Tavik Aipe. We'll get everyone in. SRU has point on this one. I'm trusting you to coordinate the search."

The man nodded. "How far?"

"Draw a ring around the city. Patrol cars blocking all roads. I want officers at the head of every mountain trail leading out of the city. Call Âmo Security. Most of them are ex-police. Use them to replace the officers at the less obvious places."

"Will that be enough?"

"Probably not." Danielsen sighed. "I think it's time to bring in the Americans."

The SRU team left the basement, leaving Danielsen with the dead teenager. He walked over to kneel beside the boy, then pulled his phone from his pocket, thinking of Kuuka and the baby.

"I'm going to be late," he said, as soon as Kuuka answered his call. Danielsen stifled a sudden rush of emotion as Kuuka asked him if everything was all right. "Not yet," he said. "But we're going to do everything we can to make it right." He looked at the dead boy as he talked. "I promise you."

Arfininngorneq

Saturday, 19th December 2043

Chapter 19

Petra stood at the back of the briefing room. She listened as Danielsen fielded questions from the journalists in the first three rows. In the wake of Greenland's independence, when the Danish officers and their families moved back to Denmark, Danielsen had stepped up, something Petra had appreciated, without really acknowledging it.

"I need to fix that," she said, as Danielsen took another question.

"What's that, ma'am?"

"Nothing." Petra turned to Tiiu and pointed at the door. "Let's get some air."

Petra took a last look at Danielsen as he pointed to the next journalist waving a microphone at him, and then followed Tiiu out of the room, all the way to the parking lot.

"It's cold, today," she said, as she stepped outside.

"You said you wanted some air."

"I did." Petra zipped her jacket and stuffed her hands in her pockets. "Run the victims by me again."

"Okay." Tiiu pulled out her phone, gripping it in the cuff of one sleeve, as she poked a finger out of the other. Her breath clouded in front of her face, pearling her eyebrows with tiny beads of ice.

"Luutivik Dalgaard and Sauli Mathiasen."

"The two old men."

"In apartment Block 3. Josef lives in Block 5."

"They died of asphyxiation."

"*Aap*, but there's no evidence of Josef ever being in their apartments. But, if they shared the same workshop, then it's not a stretch to think that they would let him in."

"But he would have to overpower them."

"Maybe. But a neighbour we spoke to yesterday, said that Luutivik liked to drink in the evening. Josef could have put a mask on his face or a chlorine cloth while Luutivik was drunk."

"Possibly." Petra nodded at Tiiu's phone. "What about Sauli?"

"Poor eyesight. Once his death was officially suspect, we pulled his records from the hospital. Maybe Josef caught him by surprise."

"Again, possible." Petra shivered and then said, "Niilsi. The boy from the market."

"We know what happened to him. He picked up a mask."

"Sara Norup was attacked, and Josef forced the mask on her face." Petra counted off on her fingers. "That's four."

"Lukka Miingu from the basement workshop makes five, ma'am. With his friend's statement, and the bottle of chlorine in Josef's apartment…"

Petra shook her head. "Circumstantial. We need hard evidence – Josef's fingerprints, a hair, anything that puts him in close physical contact with any of the victims. I had hoped the tool he stuck in the boy's neck had something."

"Clean," Tiiu said. "Like he's wearing gloves."

"Makkak Lind said she took gloves off his hand when she was in the café with him."

"We need those gloves then, ma'am."

"No, Tiiu. We need Josef." Petra nodded at the station door. "Come on. I'm freezing."

Danielsen met them at the door. He pressed his fingers to his lips and then pointed at the stairs leading to the first floor and Petra's office. Petra and Tiiu followed Danielsen through the outer office, and then stopped inside Petra's office, waiting as Danielsen closed the door.

"I need to turn the radio on," he said, brushing past Petra to the windowsill. He tapped the power button and then pressed the mute button. "Josef Filemonsen is on Kaapi Samøssen's show. Live. Now." He clicked the mute button again, and then leaned against the windowsill. Tiiu sat down on the couch, pressed against the office wall, while Petra remained standing.

"You've sent someone to the radio station?"

"Three units," Danielsen said. "As soon as I heard."

Petra dipped her head, letting her hair fall onto her shoulders as she listened.

"... there are no happy endings. Everything hurts."

Josef's voice wheezed into the office, followed by a series of sharp questions from Kaapi Samøssen.

"You hurt people," he said. *"Why?"*

"Because people hurt me."

"Not these people. Not the two old men in the

apartment."

"They were dying anyway."

"But why did you kill them?"

"I didn't touch them. They just stopped breathing."

"Like the boy in the mask," Kaapi said. *"He stopped breathing shortly after he put the mask on."*

"He chased the other boy. It's not nice to chase people. He shouldn't have done it."

"Have you been chased, Josef? Is someone chasing you?"

"Aap."

"And did the Danish woman chase you?"

"She was the teacher."

"She worked in a travel agent's, Josef."

"It doesn't matter. She was the teacher."

Danielsen pointed at the radio. "He's confessing. We have him."

"Wait," Petra said.

"And what about the boy – the teenage boy. Who was he supposed to be, Josef?"

"Nobody."

Petra lifted her head to look at the radio as the sound of Josef's breathing wheezed out of the speakers.

"But you killed him?"

"I took his teeth."

"Why?"

"If you knew, you would understand."

"Josef," Kaapi said. *"I don't think anyone understands. I don't think anyone can ever understand what you've done or why you did it."*

The sudden pause – no questions, no answers,

no breathing – turned all their heads towards the radio.

"You're just like the counsellor. You don't listen. You don't even try to understand. You could be the counsellor..."

"Send a unit to Makkak Lind's house," Petra said, clicking her fingers at Tiiu. "Go."

Danielsen pulled his phone out of his pocket as it rang. He held his mouth over the receiver a few seconds after answering the call. "Kaapi's not at the station. He's doing this live from somewhere in the city. They don't have a location. That was part of the agreement."

"What agreement?"

Danielsen pointed at the radio. "His agreement with Josef. It had to be on neutral ground."

"You mean this is face to face?"

"I think so."

Petra nodded as Danielsen pointed at the door. "Go on," she said. "I'll be here." Petra walked to her desk and grabbed the phone. She dialled as Danielsen left the office. The radio switched to commercials as Kaapi and Josef took a break. Petra tapped the side of her leg as the phone rang.

"Joshua," she said, the second he answered. "We need your help."

"This is how it works," Seabloom said, as he flashed an image from his phone onto the screen in the briefing room. "It used to be we could pinpoint a radio position through triangulation, taking readings at multiple locations and using signal strength as a guide. But Kaapi's team at the radio station is using the 8G network. It's super-fast and very strong, which is a problem, as the signal strength – in this case the bandwidth, hardly fluctuates. We can't search for the signal by prowling around the city, not even from the air. So, we physically cut into the cables, here…" He used the digital thumbs to click and point a laser to a blueprint of cables on the diagram. "And here. And in a third location, here. It uses the principle of triangulation, but instead of searching for signal strength, we're looking for identifiers. Kaapi Samøssen is, unfortunately, quite competent at masking his signature identifiers, but he's still bouncing his broadcast off the radio station's servers. It's the only thing they are broadcasting, and most of Nuuk is listening, so traffic in the city is relatively passive – listening. Giving us the opportunity to search for the active traffic – broadcasting." Seabloom lowered his hand and palmed the digital thimbles. "Sorry for the long explanation, but you wanted to know how it worked."

"Thank you," Petra said. She turned to Danielsen. "You had a question."

"How long before we have a location?"

"They're cutting into the cables now." Seabloom checked his phone. "Two out of three."

"And once they've tapped into all three?"

"Ten minutes to run the application. Provided the interview continues. If he stops talking, the chances are regular traffic will increase as people react to what they've just heard. The waters will get muddied, so to speak."

"So, we need to keep the interview going," Petra said.

"Or reduce the activity on the network."

"How?"

Seabloom gestured at the Coast Guard intelligence officer standing on his right. "Lieutenant Ford?"

"We shut down all sources of additional traffic," she said.

"You mean turn off the net?" Petra said.

"Nuuk is a small city with a localised network. It can be done, at the source – the main hub."

"Do it."

"Ma'am," Danielsen said. "Can we?"

"I don't know, but you were in the First Minister's office with me. She wanted a curfew. She wanted us to go door to door. This is basically the same thing." Petra turned to Ford and said, "What do you need?"

"Ordinarily? Permission, if we were to go by the book. But considering the time pressure."

Petra pointed at the blueprint on the screen. "Can one of your teams do it from these access points?"

"Yes, ma'am."

"Then you have my permission." Petra took a quick breath. "I'll take responsibility."

Ford glanced at Seabloom, waited for him to nod his head, and then pulled out her phone. She slipped a pair of slim headphones over her head and fired off a series of commands in rapid English – too fast for Petra and Danielsen to follow.

"Don't worry," Seabloom said. "I don't

understand what she's saying either. I'm just happy we can help. But we should get ready. This interview can't last forever."

"No," Petra said. "That's what worries me."

"Wait," Danielsen said. "What just happened?" He turned the screen of his phone towards Petra. "I've lost all signal. No Internet." He tried to dial Petra's phone. "Nothing."

"Ford?" Seabloom said, as he checked his own phone.

"They're in, and they're tracking."

"But with no network," Danielsen said. "How do we communicate? How do we coordinate the units in the city?"

"You should be able to receive, to download, but communication… Yeah, that could be a problem," Ford said.

"Aqqa," Petra said. "Stay calm. They can turn the network back on as soon as we have a fix."

"Actually, ma'am…" Ford swallowed before speaking. "We'll have to do a hard reboot. It's not possible to turn things on individually."

"You're saying that the only people who can communicate right now are your team, Kaapi and Josef Filemonsen?"

Ford took a breath. "Yes."

"Petra," Seabloom said. "I'm sorry…"

"It can wait." Petra waved her hand and then turned back to Ford. "How are you communicating with your teams?"

"On a closed network. Our own."

"And can you patch us into it?"

"No. Not without breaching security and

ringing all kinds of alarm bells in Washington." She looked at Seabloom for confirmation, continuing when he agreed. "But if we have one of your officers embedded with each team…"

"Two officers," Danielsen said. "One car each. The first officer drives to the location, while the second comes back to the station for backup."

"That puts three officers at the scene to begin with," Petra said. "That's not enough."

"It'll have to be. We're stretched pretty thin, ma'am."

"I'll put two additional Coast Guard seamen in each team," Seabloom said. He clicked his phone to make the call, then cursed at the lack of signal. "Ford, you're on the closed loop. Relay that command."

"Yes, sir."

"And in the meantime," Petra said, slumping into a chair. "We wait."

Josef's voice drifted into the briefing room as Danielsen turned up the volume on the radio.

"... I sometimes forget things. I hit my head when I was a child. The doctors said I received damage. So, I forget things. Not everything – just one thing. It's usually important. Like keys. I forgot my keys when I left my mask behind. The real mask. I had to hide it. And then the magic rebounded on me. It came back to hurt me. But I was strong. I lived. And then I had an idea, a way of making the mask even more powerful. The boy helped me with that. Now, all I have to do, is add the pieces to the mask..."

"What pieces?"

"Weren't you listening? I told you already. What the boy gave me."

"I..."

"Wasn't listening. You really are the *counsellor. You'll see. I'll help you listen."*

Petra tapped her leg. She looked at Ford. "We need to go. We need to go now!"

"Yes, ma'am. We're working on it."

Sapaat

Sunday, 20th December 2043

Chapter 20

Snow layered the Christmas lights strung across the street, frosted bulbs glowing with dull yellow cores. Danielsen drummed the steering wheel as he waited, parked alongside one of the US Coast Guard surveillance vans currently plugged into and searching Nuuk's 8G network for the location of Kaapi Samøssen's interview. He turned his head to look through the passenger window – the second time in the space of thirty seconds. Still nothing. Only the electronic blue glow of the screen reflecting in the American's glasses, lighting up his face.

"The commissioner really gave the order to lock us out of the network?" The constable sitting beside Danielsen shook his head shortly after asking the question. "I can't believe it."

"She didn't know," Danielsen said. "She took a snap decision to find Josef Filemonsen."

The constable pointed at the radio. "And now he's the only one who can talk."

"Stop talking."

"Inspector?"

"I said…" Danielsen stopped speaking at a wave from the Coast Guard van. He rolled down the window as the American seaman leaped out of the van and thrust a piece of paper in through the passenger window.

"I can't pronounce it," the American said. "But this is the address."

"*Qernertunnguit,*" the constable said.

"Got it." Danielsen snatched the paper from the constable's hand, read it twice, and then gave it back. "Get that back to the station and send the SRU to that location."

"Where are you going?"

"Where do you think?" Danielsen pointed at the door. Get out."

Danielsen shifted the SUV into first gear and peeled away from the kerb as soon as the constable was out of the car. The smart thing to do, he realised, was pick up an officer or two on the way, but listening to Josef unhinge on the radio, the number of times he accused Kaapi Samøssen of *setting him up* and *using the woman from the prison to goad him* convinced Danielsen that Kaapi's time was almost up. He accelerated, emergency lights only, no siren, flashing past the taxi rank outside Hotel Hans Egede, braking into the T-junction at the end of the road, and bumping the SUV into and through a snowbank on the opposite side of the road as he wrestled the vehicle through a patch of black ice. Danielsen recovered and turned up the radio with a flick of the button on the steering wheel.

"... you used her to get to me, to make me mad. And now I'm mad, and it's just you and me. Is that exclusive enough for you?"

Josef's language puzzled Danielsen. He seemed far more confident in Danish, stumbling to express himself in Greenlandic each time Kaapi reframed the question in their first language. But the intensity of the discourse, ratcheting up a level every few minutes, only proved what Danielsen feared, that he was going to be too late.

He spotted a patrol car in the bend before *Sipisaq Kangilleq* curved up a slight hill, away from the city centre. He braked, slowing to a stop in front of the patrol car. Danielsen wound the passenger window down and shouted for the officer behind the wheel to follow. He pulled away, wheels spinning as he accelerated, until they found purchase in a patch of grit in the bend, and the SUV powered up the hill.

There was another patrol car at the roundabout. Danielsen flashed the headlights, waving for the patrol car to pull in behind them. He braked into the roundabout, accelerated out of it, then looked in the mirror, settling in his seat and feeling more confident as he saw the two patrol cars following.

He slowed at the next roundabout, then took the exit for *Qernertunnguanut*, slowing even more as he led the column of police cars up the hill and into the residential area – semidetached wooden houses, the kind Kuuka hoped they could move into before the baby was born. Danielsen slowed to a stop, listened to the radio to check that Kaapi was still broadcasting, that he was still alive, and then got out of the car. The two officers, one constable and a sergeant, joined Danielsen on the street.

"First road on the right," Danielsen said. "Second house on the left. He pulled his pistol from his holster and checked the magazine, nodding as the two officers did the same. "We'll drive up to

Timerlia." He pointed to the road leading to the houses on the right. Most of the houselights were lit, not unusual in the winter dark, even in the very early hours of the morning. "People are asleep, or listening to the radio," he said. "But I want one of you to park at the turning."

"I'll do that," said the younger of the two men."

Danielsen nodded at the sergeant. "That leaves you and me to cordon off the street, Gustav. Is that okay?"

"We're not going in?" Gustav hiked his thumb over his shoulder at the nearest patrol car. "I've been listening to the radio. He's ramping up."

"And if we go in without backup," Danielsen said, "we might not be able to stop him. *Naamik*," he said, shaking his head. "We wait."

Gustav slipped his pistol back into his holster and nodded that he was ready.

"Once we get there, we wait outside the house. Turn your lights off before we enter the street. Keep the engine running – they're quiet enough."

Danielsen gave each man a last look, then jogged back to his car. He pulled away gently from the kerb, turning right onto *Timerlia*, and slowing to a stop just before he reached the house. He listened to the radio, then wound the window down so he could hear it from the street. Gustav was waiting outside the car as Danielsen got out.

"No lights on the ground floor," Gustav said, pointing at the house.

"Bedroom and bathroom lights are on," Danielsen said. "We need to look around the back." He paused at a fresh outburst from Josef.

"...if you want to live, you'll bring her to me. Then we can swap her life for yours. The people should be happy with that. I can repent my sins..."

"You know," Gustav said. "I don't remember hearing Kaapi's voice for a while. This sounds like a monologue."

Danielsen bit his lip as he thought about it. If Josef was just preaching to the microphone, it could mean that Kaapi was incapacitated. *Or worse,* he thought, with another glance at the lights in the upstairs bedroom.

"Maybe we can't wait," Gustav said. "I think we have to go in."

"And if Kaapi dies when we do?"

"He could be dead already. What's the difference?"

Danielsen pressed his finger into Gustav's chest. "There's a world of difference. Don't let me hear you talk like that again."

"*Aap*, Inspector."

"Okay." Danielsen took a moment to look at the house. He brushed a clump of snow from his hair as he contemplated the best way into the house. He looked back at the road, saw the shadow of the constable's SUV at the turning, but no sign of backup. He pulled his pistol from his holster and nodded for Gustav to do the same. "We go in front and back. This type of house has the stairs at the front. I'll wait for you there once you've come in from the back."

"We're going to make some noise, Inspector."

"Unavoidable." Danielsen turned his head towards the car. He listened for Josef on the radio, and then slapped Gustav on the shoulder. "Go."

New snow provided a soft carpet for them to tread on. Danielsen led the way to the front door, then pulled Gustav close to whisper in his ear that he will count to thirty before going in the front door. Gustav nodded and then slipped around the back of the house.

Danielsen felt the cold pinch the tips of his ears, and soft thumps of snow of his head. He started counting. He thought of Kuuka during the first five seconds, their son, and what would happen if Josef got the upper hand as he entered the house.

He *should* wait for backup.

A crack of wood and the splinter of glass turned his head. He took a step back from the door to look up, before realising that the noise came from the back of the house.

Gustav, going through the back door.

Danielsen reached for the door handle, held his breath, and hoped that the door was unlocked. He froze at a clicking sound on the other side of the door. Danielsen stepped back, raised his pistol in a two-handed grip, and then frowned as the door opened inwards, and Gustav peered around the door.

"I could have shot you," Danielsen whispered.

Gustav nodded and then motioned for Danielsen to step inside the house. He pressed his lips to Danielsen's ear and said, "It's clear downstairs."

Danielsen took the lead, climbing the stairs, his pistol raised, eyes darting to either side. Gustav followed just a step behind him. Danielsen thought about telling him to wait, to put some space between them, but then he reached the top step, saw the light from the bedroom filtering around the frame and onto the landing. He pointed to the left-hand side, waited for Gustav to take that position, and then moved to the door, reaching for the handle.

Josef's voice sounded exactly like it did on the radio. Danielsen frowned as he pressed his ear to the door. He sounded *exactly* the same. The same tinny distortion, nothing natural.

He turned the handle with his left hand, holding the pistol in his right, just in front of his chin, as he opened the door.

Josef's voice grew louder, but no clearer.

Danielsen pushed the door wider, slowly slipping into the room with Gustav right behind him. He felt the sergeant's right hand on his left shoulder, surprising himself as he realised Gustav must be holding his pistol in the other hand. His left.

Focus.

Josef continued to rant, more about the *woman from the prison* and an *exchange – her for Kaapi*. But he could only do that, Danielsen realised, if he wasn't there.

Danielsen pushed the door back and stepped fully into the room. He saw the desk first, the computer screen and the live feed from a camera. He saw Josef's face – rather, he saw the black mask, creased with lines gouged into the sooty surface. Behind Josef was another figure, bound to a chair, head lolling to one side.

"Kaapi?" Gustav said, as he followed Danielsen

into the room.

"*Imaqa*. Hard to tell with that mask on."

"Then he's dead already."

Danielsen took a step closer to the screen, ignoring Josef as he continued his rant, focusing instead on the man on the chair. He saw the man's chest rise and then fall, just enough to allow Danielsen to relax, if only for a moment.

"He's alive," he said, slipping his pistol back into his holster. "For now."

Gustav moved to the window at the sound of vehicles pulling up in the street outside the house. He tapped Danielsen on the shoulder and said something about going downstairs. Danielsen said nothing. He pulled out the chair in front of the desk and sat down, staring at Josef in his mask, struggling to pull his eyes away from it. He didn't see the man, only the mask. He barely heard the words. One part of his brain wondered if they even meant anything, if they were simply words, that the mask was the most important thing.

"Aqqa?"

Danielsen turned as Petra stepped into the room. Two SRU officers in full tactical gear came with her.

"He must have a location beacon or something," Danielsen said, gesturing at the computer with a wave of his hand. "So we think it's coming from here, but it's been routed from somewhere else."

"We'll process everything," Petra said. "We'll find out where he is."

"Right," Danielsen said. He stood up and turned

to look at Petra. "You heard what he wants?"

"Yes," she said. "He wants Natuk." Petra waited a beat and then looked Danielsen in the eye. "The First Minister has already decided to give her to him."

"And you're going to let her?"

"Yes. But I had one condition, to which the First Minister agreed." Petra gave Danielsen a thin smile and said, "I'm going with her."

"Commissioner…"

"Stop, Aqqa. It's decided. It's my punishment for all my sins, including shutting down the network. It's also going to be my last official act as commissioner." Petra took a step forwards and pressed her hand into Danielsen's. "Congratulations. You will be the next, and in my opinion, the best commissioner to take Greenland into an independent future. But first," she said, with a nod to the computer screen. "We have to deal with him."

Ataasinngorneq

Monday, 21st December 2043

Chapter 21

"Bring up that last image."

Petra curled her hands around a large mug of tea, blowing ripples on the surface as Danielsen continued the briefing he had started the night before. His face was lined with fatigue and stress, Petra even thought he had lost weight.

"There," Danielsen said. "The mouth of the mask. Teeth."

Petra saw them, then turned to look over her shoulder as Professor Korniliu Duko shuffled from his seat to the screen for a closer look.

"Professor?" Danielsen said.

Korniliu climbed the two steps onto the stage in front of the screen and pointed at the teeth in Josef's mask. "He must have glued them in place," he said. "But that's not important." Korniliu reached up to tap the screen, placing his finger on the forehead of the mask, right between the eyes. "It's what the teeth have done to him up here that counts."

"Can you explain that, Professor," Petra said. "In English please," she added with a nod to Seabloom sitting to her right.

"With pleasure," Korniliu said. "I've listened to the recording of Josef's interview. You have all noted his aggressive tone, particularly towards the end of the interview. This doesn't fit with the Josef

Makkak Lind described. Nor the reports from the school, and those Tiiu brought back from the children's home. But it suggests that Josef *feels* stronger now than he did before. The woman who saw him at the church…" Korniliu's forehead creased as if he was trying to remember something. "I'm sorry, I don't remember her name. But she mentioned nothing about teeth. Then your report about the boy…"

"Lukka Miingu," Danielsen said.

Petra caught the shadow that passed across Danielsen's eyes as he said the boy's name. Clearly, finding the boy had left a mark on Greenland's next police commissioner.

And no wonder, she thought. She smiled as Danielsen caught her eye, and then turned her attention back to Korniliu.

"If we assume that these are the boy's teeth, and when we look at the material Josef was reading in his apartment – the books. It's safe to say that he believes in the magic of the mask. He also believes he has made it stronger. This makes *him* stronger. At least in his own eyes."

"Excuse me, Professor, you're not suggesting Josef Filemonsen has superpowers?"

Petra looked over her shoulder to see Pipaluk Uutaaq standing at the back of the room and wondered when she had arrived.

"No, First Minister. He doesn't have superpowers, but he thinks he does. It is my belief that if you remove the mask from the man, because he believes so strongly, then he will also be weakened once the mask is taken from him."

"And destroyed," Danielsen said.

"*Naamik*," Korniliu said. "You mustn't destroy it. Rather, you must use it against him. If it is destroyed, then he is safe. He is more likely to surrender if you possess the mask."

"Excuse me once more, Professor. But you are a historian, not a psychologist. Is that correct?" Pipaluk tucked her hands into the slim pockets of her tailored suit, twisting her lips into a smirk as she waited for Korniliu to respond.

"I am not a psychologist."

"Then tell me why you are all spending so much time on this aspect of the case, when surely a bullet will be far more effective, if, as you say, he does not have superpowers."

"Because, First Minister," Petra said. "Our job is to protect life, including Josef Filemonsen's."

"After he has taken so many lives already?"

"Yes. Perhaps even more so, because of that. If we're going to help the families of the people he has killed, then we must capture him, alive." Petra pointed at the screen. "Understanding what the mask means to Josef could make all the difference."

"I guess we will find out," Pipaluk said. Her lips parted as if she was about to say more, only to freeze as the door opened and two heavily armed SRU officers entered the room with two more following them. Shuffling in short, chained steps between the four men was Natuk Petersen.

"You started without me," she said, as one of the SRU officers guided her into a seat.

Danielsen straightened his back and faced Natuk. "You know why you're here?"

Natuk turned to look at Pipaluk, then Petra. She smiled at Seabloom and then winked at Tiiu standing in the opposite corner of the room. "I know it's important," she said. "And it has something to do with the masked avenger there." She raised her cuffed wrists and pointed at the screen. "Your men let slip that he had asked for me."

"And I wonder why," Danielsen said.

"Aqqa," Petra said. She shook her head, then worked her way along the row of chairs to the front of the room. "Tiiu. Next slide, please."

Tiiu clicked the digital thimbles on her finger and thumb and flashed a map onto the screen.

"This is the top of *Nuup Kangerlua*, Nuuk fjord," Petra said. "Tiiu." Petra waited for Tiiu to highlight a natural bay on the western shores of the fjord. "I asked Constable Mikkiki to talk to the staff at the children's home. She went through their records, and we know that this location was used as a summer camp around the time when Josef lived at the children's home. He visited it twice. Unfortunately, the second time proved to be a tragic experience, and Josef was sexually abused at the camp by one of the staff members. At least, that's what we think. The staff member in question was employed as a counsellor but left at the end of the same summer for a job in Denmark. This is thirteen years ago. Josef would have been nine years old. The other staff knew something was wrong, but it took him a long time to tell them anything about it." Petra turned to Korniliu, and said, "We know that the camp means something to Josef, but Professor Duko has more information."

"The location," Korniliu said, "was used as a winter camp many years ago. It is recorded in the same books that we know Josef has read. And, once again…" Korniliu looked at Pipaluk. "Because we know that Josef believes in the power of masks and Greenland magic, then he might also see the old winter camp as a place of power."

"Makkak Lind knew Josef when he was in school," Petra said. "From what she told us, it would appear that there have been some tragic events in Josef's past, events which he has tried to purge through the deaths of his victims. Some of them, at least. Specifically, we know he was chased a lot as a boy. His first victim – the first person killed with a mask – was a young boy, perhaps the same age as those who chased him. The Danish woman, possibly, might be a substitute for the Danish teacher Makkak says treated Josef unkindly in school. It's possible that Josef thinks he can purge from his memory the worst act he suffered at the place where it occurred."

"The winter camp," Danielsen said. "Josef has yet to confirm where he wants us to bring Natuk, but there are cabins at that location, and the radio station has confirmed that Kaapi Samøssen has visited the camp twice during recent summers."

"And the poison masks," Pipaluk said. "What is the significance of them?"

"Tiiu?" Petra said, with a nod to the young constable.

"First Minister," Tiiu said, drawing a soft snigger from Natuk as she dipped her head in a deferential bow. "Makkak Lind also told us about an incident when Josef passed out." Tiiu coughed to clear her throat, and said, "When he was forced to piss on a bleach block."

"He passed out?" Pipaluk said.

"He was a small boy. There was a chemical reaction with the…"

"Yes, thank you, Constable," Pipaluk said. "I get it." She turned back to Petra. "And this explains the masks?"

"It's one explanation," Petra said. "Together with the supernatural element."

Natuk's chains rattled as she raised her hands. "And where do I come in? Is he pissed because I called him a coward?"

"There's that possibility," Petra said. "Or…"

"Maybe I planned the whole thing," Natuk said. She looked over her shoulder at Pipaluk and smiled. "Maybe I found Josef before I was caught, planted a seed in his tortured brain, then activated him, like a sleeper agent."

"Enough!" Petra walked towards Natuk, stopping just in front of her and taking a breath as Natuk turned her head slowly to stare at her. "We don't have time for games, Natuk. You've had your fun. This is serious now."

"Like it was serious with my brother, you mean?"

"Ooqi was a good officer," Petra said. "I've always said that. He was manipulated. You both were."

Natuk gritted her teeth. "You killed him, *Commissioner*."

"And I'll admit to that as many times as you

need me to. But no one in this room has anything good to say about you or your brother. No one in Greenland." Petra kept her eyes fixed on Natuk as she talked. "But if you do this one thing, then you could change that. You could change the way people talk about you, and if you don't care about your own name, then think about Ooqi. Think what you could do for him."

"And what about you, Commissioner?" Natuk said."What's in it for you?"

"This will be my last job as commissioner. I'm retiring after this."

"Retiring?" Natuk snorted. "They finally figured out your heart isn't in it, eh?"

"Yes, something like that."

"Or have you been pronounced mentally unfit?" Natuk licked her bottom lip. She raised her voice. "Has she told you about the video? About how she can't sleep at night because Constable Maratse has come back from the grave with a secret?"

"Natuk," Petra whispered. "Don't."

"No?" Natuk lowered her voice. "We all have our secrets. If you want my help, I'll need something in return."

"I can't release you, Natuk."

"We'll see. Maybe when the time comes, you might want to." Natuk waved Petra closer with her fingers, lowering her voice to a whisper. "You see, I think I know where that video was taken."

"What?"

"I know where to go." Natuk smiled. "I can take you there."

"Natuk…"

"If you want my help." Natuk shrugged. "You'll figure it out." Petra took a step back, catching her breath as Natuk lifted her head, and said, "I need to use the toilet. You don't need me here. Just take me to the bathroom and then put me on the boat." She looked at Petra. "I'm ready when you are."

The rattle of Natuk's chains hung in the air for a few seconds after the SRU team escorted her from the room. The rattling continued down the hall, fading as the SRU marched her to the nearest toilet. Petra took a breath, sat down, and then gestured for Danielsen to continue.

"We have a plan for the operation," he said. "Assuming that Josef will make some demands about who and how many people will bring Natuk to him, we're going to have two teams. Constable Mikkiki will escort Commissioner Jensen, together with two SRU officers guarding Natuk. Commander Seabloom has promised the use of a Coast Guard helicopter and a strike team. They'll take up position nearby, ready to move in at Commissioner Jensen's command. I will remain in Nuuk and coordinate the operation from this room."

"You can do that?" Pipaluk asked. "What about the network? You couldn't even make a phone call a few hours ago."

Seabloom stood up and said, "My people assure me they will have the network fully restored within the hour. We're working with city technicians, and we are truly sorry about what happened."

"Hmm," Pipaluk said. "I expect regular updates." She looked at Danielsen before leaving the room.

"If I may," Korniliu said. "Provided you don't think I will get in the way, I would like to join the commissioner's team, if she will have me?"

"I don't think that's such a good idea."

"Actually, Aqqa," Petra said. "I think Professor Duko may provide valuable insight. I would be pleased to have him come with us."

"Thank you, Commissioner." Korniliu dipped his head in a gentle bow, not dissimilar to Tiiu's.

Petra excused herself. "If there's nothing else. I'll get ready."

"Commissioner," Seabloom called out as Petra left the room. "Petra?"

Petra walked into the corridor and kept going, past the stairs leading to her office, on to the main entrance and out into the parking lot. She took a deep breath of freezing air, felt the cold grip her lungs, and then coughed, stuffing her hands into her jacket pockets as she walked across the parking lot to the cultural centre.

Piitalaat…

"Not now, David. Please. Not now."

She held the door to *Katuaq* for a young mother pushing her child in a pram and then followed her inside. She bought a strong coffee, hoping the kick would push the video out of her head. But it was too late. It had already started.

Marlunngorneq

Tuesday, 22nd December 2043

Chapter 22

Petra stood in the bow of the small fishing trawler, clutching the side of a plastic fish bin, as she focused on the distant horizon. The sea was black under a winter night sky, littered with small icebergs and growlers, big enough to force the skipper to sail around them, while letting the smaller lumps of brash ice clink and bump along the length of the hull. Petra drew small, stepped breaths, fighting back waves of nausea as the trawler ploughed through the swell of the sea deeper and deeper into *Nuup Kangerlua.* The rest of the crew, including Natuk and the two SRU officers sent to guard her, were inside, warm in the wheelhouse. Petra took another series of breaths, letting her mind wander, thinking through recent events – personal and professional – in the lulls between waves and bouts of seasickness.

Seabloom had been the first to comment on the trawler as they prepared to leave, telling her, "The Coast Guard has more than one helicopter, you know?"

"But we don't want to spook him."

"Then take one of the police cutters."

"Can't. Same reason."

"Then how else can I help you, Petra?"

"You've helped me so much already," she had

said, thinking about the Saturday in her apartment, how much she had enjoyed his attention, before gently, reluctantly, asking him to leave before things *got too serious*. He had taken it harder than she had expected.

It's a sign, she thought, squirming her feet on the deck as the bow rose over the crest of the next wave. *Slow it down. Small steps. If it's meant to be...*

She laughed in the bow, ignoring the churn in her stomach for the moment as she wondered how many clichés she could apply to her personal life.

Personal life.

The short voyage into the fjord, regardless of the police operation to apprehend Josef Filemonsen, was just another step on a longer personal journey. Petra steeled herself in the face of a set of waves lifting the port side of the boat, gripping the fish bin, squaring her feet, bending her knees, and quashing the nagging thoughts she had regarding Natuk's intentions. She thought about Iiluuna and Quaa instead, going through her will in her mind, one last time, as she ticked off what she hoped were comprehensive instructions that would benefit them both after she was gone.

In the event that I die... Not when I die.

Another wave, a blast of freezing spray in her face. Petra shivered, then dug deep for the resolve she knew she needed to tackle the last few personal concerns before they reached the winter campground.

Piitalaat...

"Yes, David," she said, speaking into the wind,

perhaps even to it. He was part of nature, after all, not just in her head, but in the air, the land, the sea, and the ice. "You left me a puzzle."

It was not my intention.

"I know, but it's still a puzzle. I want to know – I *need* to know who else you have loved, why you loved them, and how finding them might just bring something of you back to me." Petra wiped a warm tear from her cold, salt-stained cheek. "I thought I was ready to move on. Now…" Petra felt her fingers cramp in the cold. She shivered. "I'm not so sure." She looked over her shoulder at the wheelhouse, saw Natuk staring back at her. "And I don't know what to do."

Let me go.

"I thought I could," she said. "I really did."

This isn't healthy.

"Okay, that's me speaking." Petra lurched forward as a wave caught her unawares. "Enough," she said. "I need to get warm."

Be careful, Piitalaat. Promise me.

"I promise."

Petra used the fish bins and the railings to walk back to the wheelhouse, leapfrogging her way along the deck. She stopped at the wheelhouse ladder, sealing all remaining personal thoughts in a part of her mind for later, when she had more time. She gripped the plastic-coated handholds on either side of the ladder and climbed. The door to the wheelhouse opened and Tiiu helped her inside, guiding her to the table where Korniliu pressed a mug of hot tea into her hands.

"We thought you'd never come in," he said.

"I don't sail well. Some times are better than others. This is not one of those times."

Natuk turned her head, her forehead wrinkled with a curious look as she tuned in to the conversation at the table. Her eyes never left Petra.

"Professor," Petra said. "I want you to stay with Tiiu at all times. Is that clear?"

"Very clear."

"And Tiiu?"

"Ma'am?"

"You will be the link between us and Inspector Danielsen back in Nuuk. Stay on the radio. If the radio fails, use the one on the boat."

"Is he going to give himself up, ma'am?"

"I don't know what he's going to do. We'll just have to find out." Petra swapped a look with Natuk, curious that she seemed calm, focused. *Professional,* Petra thought. *She's always been professional; in everything, she's done.*

The skipper of the chartered trawler announced they were close. He slowed down, as they had agreed before leaving Nuuk, steering the boat towards a second dock, a little to the south of the campsite.

Petra joined him at the wheel, standing next to Natuk as she looked at the lights in the cabin windows. There were three cabins, and the lights were lit in all of them.

"Smart," Natuk said. "We'll have to search all three."

"Not you," Petra said. "You're staying on the boat. Visible on deck, sure, but you're not to set one foot on land. Do you understand?"

"Won't that depend on Josef? He's the one who wanted me here."

"But that doesn't mean he tells us what to do. Not anymore. It stops now. We stop him here."

The trawler bumped against the black wood of the old dock. The sea-bloated timbers creaked and groaned as the skipper used a little power, pushing the hull against the wooden supports, compensating for the suck and surge of the changing tide. Petra checked her pistol as they waited on the deck. One of the SRU men secured the trawler with a line he snaked over the gunwale, curling it around a thick wooden pole at the bow, and then another at the stern. He held out his hand to help Petra onto the dock, then again for Tiiu and the professor.

"It's slippery," he said, raising his voice above the surf and the wind.

"We'll be careful." Petra led the way along the narrow dock and onto the shore. She turned back to help the others, avoiding Natuk's gaze as she watched them from the wheelhouse.

"You're sure you don't want one of us to come with you?" The SRU officer fidgeted at the end of the dock. "You don't know what he's capable of."

"But we know what *she* is capable of." Petra pointed at the wheelhouse. "Keep an eye on Natuk. Those are your orders. If Josef wants to see her, we'll let you know. Then you bring her onto the deck." Petra's jacket flapped in the wind and she zipped the collar to her chin. "We'll take it from there."

The SRU officer held out his hand, shaking

Petra's when she took it. "Good luck, Commissioner."

Petra watched as he jogged back to the boat and then led her party forward.

Tiiu questioned the professor as they picked their way along the shoreline. "You said a more powerful shaman could turn another shaman's power against him."

"*Aap.*"

"I was just wondering," Tiiu said, gripping Korniliu's arm as a sudden gust of wind buffeted them. "Are you a shaman?"

Korniliu shook his head. "I'm sorry, Constable. I am not."

"That's a shame. I kind of hoped you were."

"That's all right. But I wouldn't worry," Korniliu said. "Josef isn't a shaman either."

"But I thought…"

"Reading about magic, rituals, and masks, doesn't make someone a shaman. They have to be picked, and they have to choose it. Often it would be a child who showed some aptitude for communicating with spirits – perhaps they were seen daydreaming, even talking to themselves, just enough to catch the shaman's interest. There were trials and tests, and the shaman would have to learn every bone in his or her body. To do that, each bone would be broken. Figuratively speaking." Korniliu slowed as they neared the first cabin. He lowered his voice in a sudden lull in the wind. "Of course, there are many ways and practices. But Josef has taken a shortcut. I don't deny he has taken the time and put a lot of thought into his mask. But, as Natuk said in her interview, he is using the same mask all the time. History shows that it's dangerous to do so."

"Let's hope so," Petra said, as she brought them to a stop, turning her head slightly at the sound of a generator rumbling somewhere close by. "This is as far as the two of you go."

"Ma'am?"

"I'm going to go look for Josef."

"Alone?"

"It's okay," Petra said, forcing a smile. "I'm not completely alone. You're here. The SRU is on the boat. And…"

Piitalaat.

Petra curled a loose strand of hair behind her ear as Maratse's voice echoed inside her head.

"Let's just say, I have backup when I need it, and an American helicopter full of guns just a few minutes away. Although," she said, as the falling snow thickened. "This could be a problem."

"Perhaps we should…"

"No, Tiiu. Stay here. Stay with the professor. Keep him safe."

Petra turned before Tiiu could respond. She walked towards the first cabin, shielding her eyes from the light streaming out of the windows as she approached, only to pause as she spotted something further along the beach.

The cabin light stretched across the small boulders, rocks, and pebbles to a chair pressed into the sand. The man bound to it wore one of Josef's masks, fastened to his head with an elastic band. Petra approached, one hand on the holster at her hip. She unsnapped the strap, teasing her hand around the pistol grip as she studied the area, the man in the chair, the shadows between the cabins.

The surf deposited small lumps of ice on the beach, close to the man's feet. Petra checked her phone, noting that it was close to midnight, and that the days were ticking by, closer and closer to Christmas.

"It'll be over before then," she whispered. "One way or another."

The wind licked the words from her lips, leaving salt and the soft brush of thick snowflakes in its wake.

Petra approached the man in the chair, forcing herself to check the background, to not focus on the man's body. If her attention was fixed solely on the man, and Josef got the better of her, then there would be more blood, more bodies, and a sad eulogy for Danielsen to deliver at her funeral.

Piitalaat.

"Yes?"

Focus.

Petra took another step closer to the body, flicking the larger lumps of ice to one side with the reinforced toecaps of her boots.

She stopped again. Close enough now to see that the man was breathing, but also that he was cold, and that his jeans and tie-dyed t-shirt were not enough to keep him warm. Whether the mask on his face was poisoned didn't matter, he would die of hypothermia if Petra didn't help him.

Petra let go of her pistol, sliding it back into the holster, as she reached out for the man. She started to speak, to call out his name, only for the words to catch in her throat at the sound of shots fired behind her.

Petra turned to see the flicker of muzzle flashes on the deck of the trawler, and then nothing, as the trawler's lights flicked off, and the echo of gunfire was absorbed in the snow.

"Commissioner," Tiiu shouted.

Petra peered through the snow, squinting in the light from the cabins, staring back along the beach at Tiiu and the professor, as they lurched forward, stumbling ahead of a woman carrying one of the SRU's submachine guns.

"Natuk," Petra said, just as the cabin lights were extinguished, and the soft, persistent *thud thud thud* of the generator was silenced.

Pingasunngorneq

Wednesday, 23rd December 2043

Chapter 23

It should have been clear from the start. Petra chided herself for underestimating Natuk Petersen. Had she not used Greenland masks in her campaign? Less than a year ago, Natuk had almost brought the city to its knees. Unless Josef Filemonsen had been out of the country, or comatose for the first six days of the year, he would have struggled not to see the effect a mask could have upon the people of Greenland. It was in Greenland's cultural DNA. It was in the Greenlanders' blood – Josef's *and* Natuk's.

Petra raised her hands as Natuk approached. She took a step further up the beach, conscious that she had yet to remove Kaapi's mask, concerned that he needed to get inside, that they should call the helicopter, and that Josef was still loose, close by, perhaps. It was difficult to tell. Petra struggled to imagine what his endgame was, especially now that Natuk carried one of the SRU's submachine guns.

"Don't worry about your boys," Natuk said. She ordered Tiiu and Korniliu to drop to their knees on the beach. She tucked Tiiu's pistol into the waistband of her cargo trousers and slung the MP5 casually across her chest. "I left them cuffed on the beach with the skipper. Under a blanket, of course."

"You overpowered them."

"Of course," Natuk said.

"And you've thought it all through?"

Natuk pulled a set of keys from her pocket and twirled them around her fingers. "The keys to the kingdom," she said. "Or whatever the boat is called."

"*Aarluk*," Tiiu said. "The killer whale."

"I do like this one," Natuk said, stroking Tiiu's hair before pocketing her keys. "Perhaps I'll keep her?"

"Whatever we do, Natuk, we have to get Kaapi inside."

"What *we* do? Commissioner, really, you need to reset, and get used to the new order of things. And, while you're doing that, you can toss your pistol over to me." Natuk drew an arc in the sand with her boot. "Can you see that? Toss it there."

Petra slid her pistol out of the holster. Natuk kept the MP5 slung and Tiiu's pistol in her trousers. She held her hands at her sides. Petra knew it was for show, part of the game, and that Natuk could draw the pistol like an American gunslinger if she wanted to.

She probably wants to. It's what she's waiting for.

Petra tossed the pistol onto the beach and imagined the disappointed look on Natuk's face.

"Let me check if it is Kaapi," Petra said, gesturing at the man in the chair.

"It's him," Natuk said. "I spotted his shirt all the way from the trawler."

"Then let me get him inside."

"No can do." Natuk bent down to pick up

Petra's gun and then used it to point to a spot further up the mountain behind the cabins. "See that flicker of light?"

Petra turned to look.

"I noticed it when the cabin lights were turned off. Josef is playing a game, Commissioner, and he wants us to join in. Come on. We'll leave Kaapi in the capable hands of Constable Mikkiki and her learned friend."

"It could be a trap, Natuk."

"Really? I hadn't thought of that. But I do hope so. I've been stuck behind bars for so long, I'm so bored, Petra, like you wouldn't believe."

"You're being dramatic. It doesn't suit you."

"I suppose it doesn't." Natuk walked the short distance between them, holding her hand out as she reached Petra. "Phone. Radio."

Petra slapped her phone into Natuk's hand and said, "I don't have a radio."

"Fine. But can you live without your phone?"

"Yes."

"Of course, you can. You've already memorised Maratse's video. But we can talk about that as we walk." Natuk stuffed Petra's phone into the cargo pocket of her trousers and then gestured for Petra to follow her. "Cheer up, Commissioner. We're going on an adventure."

The light above them flickered in the snow, sometimes closer, other times farther away, as they twisted and stumbled up the granite path scored into the mountainside. Natuk slowed at each turn, listening for sounds of a trap or an ambush, before waving Petra on and up the mountain. The snow continued to fall, heavier still.

Danielsen will have ordered the boat to leave Nuuk by now, she thought. *Maybe even earlier. I hope it was earlier.*

Natuk cut into Petra's thoughts with a confession. "I know who sent the video of Maratse."

Petra stopped on the track. "What?"

"*The* video. The one you can't get out of your mind."

"Who sent it, Natuk?"

"My brother. Ooqi." Natuk grinned in the grey light beneath the snow clouds. "That's how I know it's real. He left his mark on it. You wouldn't notice, but the shadow on the mountains in the distance, behind the fishermen – that's where it is. A subtle skull, just a shade lighter than the shadow."

"I never saw that."

"You're focused on the foreground. Focused on Maratse. I've never met him. Couldn't care less. So I saw more than you." Natuk's tone changed as she continued. "And that's when I knew Ooqi cared about you."

"I don't understand."

"I don't expect you to. But Ooqi said good things about you. He liked the way you treated him. He probably found the video and set up a dead man's switch."

"What do you mean?"

"In the event something happened to Ooqi, if he wasn't able to stop it, the video would be sent to you on a certain date."

"A year after Maratse died."

"*Aap*."

"Why?"

"You'd have to ask Ooqi. But…"

Petra waited for the usual barb from Natuk, reminding her she was the one to shoot and kill her twin brother.

"Honestly, Commissioner, that video is the only thing keeping you alive."

"Because it came from your brother?"

"Because my brother cared enough about you to send it. He's keeping you alive, from beyond the grave." Natuk shrugged in the dark. "Believe it or not, I respect that. I might not know what Ooqi intends for you to do with it, but he wanted you to have it. That's enough for me. At least, it's enough for now."

"Meaning you'll kill me later once your curiosity has been satisfied?"

"Petra," Natuk said. "I took out two SRU officers, your constable, and two more men, now that we're counting. I could have killed you earlier, I'm saying I might kill you later, but for now, I'm letting you live."

"That's very gracious of you," Petra said, wondering if Natuk could see her sneer in the dark.

"You're welcome. But now…" Natuk pointed up the mountain. "I think we had better keep going. That light is fading."

They walked the rest of the way in silence, slowing as they drew closer to the light. Natuk shifted her grip on the submachine gun, tucking the folded stock into her shoulder as she looked over the sight. Petra watched as Natuk scanned the trail, her head fixed in a straight line as if it was attached on a tight lead to the barrel. Natuk stopped and dropped to one knee, hissing for Petra to do the same.

"There's a body ahead," she whispered. "Wearing a mask."

"What kind of mask?"

"The original," Natuk said. "The body is not moving. I'm going to check it out."

Petra followed in Natuk's shadow, straining her eyes in the scant grey light from the clouds above them reflecting on the snow. Natuk stopped again as she reached the body's feet. She trained the barrel of the MP5 on the body's chest and kicked the nearest ankle. The mask rocked as the vibration travelled through the body, but no sound or movement followed. Petra stepped around Natuk.

"Careful, Commissioner."

The mask grinned at Petra with its four bloody teeth. She thought of Danielsen, and the image of Lukka's bloody mouth as he lay on the floor in the basement. Petra reached out to touch the mask, pausing just a thumb's length from the chin, ready to lift it, and yet suddenly aware of a prickling on her skin.

"It's just a mask," Natuk said.

Petra knew it, even so, she wasn't sure.

She held her breath and pinched the bottom of the mask, lifting it, curious to see Josef's face. The sling around Natuk's chest clicked as she shifted her stance.

"That," Natuk said, as Petra lifted the mask. "Is Kaapi Samøssen."

"You said…"

Natuk swore. "They were his clothes. I made a mistake. He played us."

Petra pressed her fingers against Kaapi's skin, searching for a pulse. "His skin is cold," she said.

"He's dead, Petra." Natuk lowered the MP5, cursing again as she looked back down the mountain. "We have to go. I know where he is."

"Give me my phone," Petra said. She dialled the second she unlocked the screen, tapping her fingers on her leg as she waited for Tiiu to pick up. "No answer," she said. "I'll call Aqqa."

"No time," Natuk said, grabbing the phone from Petra's hand. "Come on."

Petra zipped Josef's mask inside her jacket and followed Natuk down the mountain path.

Natuk led the way, boots sliding in patches of gravel, slipping on smooth stretches of ice. She fell. They both did. They picked each other up, then raced on, ignoring the scuffs on their shins, the dull, heavy impact of granite on their knees. Natuk cried out after a longer fall, biting back the pain and drawing blood from her lip as Petra helped her to her feet.

"I'm all right," she said. "Just mad."

"Because you're hurt?"

"Because he tricked me." Natuk stumbled forward. "The little prick. He played me from the trawler."

"He played us both."

"But I'm the one he fooled. I'm the one he led up the mountain. And it's your people who are going to suffer for it."

"That's up to you, Natuk. This isn't over yet."

The last stretch of the track was steep but ice-free. Petra ran down it, charging onto the thick bed of Arctic grasses poking out of the snow. She reached for Natuk's arm, pulling her along the last few metres towards the cabins.

They slowed at the sound of the generator and then stopped as Josef's voice whined out of speakers in each of the cabins.

"It's his interview," Natuk said, flicking her gaze from one cabin to the next.

"Three different parts of the same interview." Petra held out her hand. "Pistol and phone, Natuk."

"I don't know…"

"Then one of us will die here, probably. That seems to be his intention – to confuse and disarm us. But I'm not going into any of these cabins without a gun."

Petra waited, palm outstretched, until Natuk placed her phone first, and then, hesitantly, Petra's gun.

Petra slipped her phone into her pocket and then pointed at the cabin on the right. "That's yours," she said. "I'll take the one in the middle. We meet at the last one."

Natuk nodded and then pointed at the empty chair on the beach. Clumps of ice clustered around the chair legs. "High tide," she said.

Josef's voice cut into the night, rising above the wind as someone turned the volume up inside one cabin, and then, a half minute later, down in the next one.

"He's moving between the cabins," Petra said.

Natuk shifted her grip on the MP5, and stalked towards the cabin on her right, just as Josef's voice reached a new distorted high. Petra ignored it and turned to the cabin on her left.

She held her pistol in a two-handed grip in front of her, keeping the iron sights of the pistol level with her eyes, just as Natuk had done. She stepped onto the deck of the cabin, felt her foot slide on the icy surface, recovered, and then walked towards the front door.

Josef's voice was louder now, raging in her ears.

Petra reached the door, turned the handle, and stepped inside.

The lights flickered on and off, casting a strobe effect across the room, throwing a shaft of light across Tiiu's body, the blood on her hand, and the mask on her face.

"Tiiu," Petra said, taking another step into the cabin.

Josef's interview ended with a flick of a switch, and the cabin was plunged into darkness.

Sisamanngorneq

Thursday, 24th December 2043

Christmas Eve

Chapter 24

Petra's nostrils prickled at the smell of something like ash, but oilier. She pressed one hand to her chest, felt the mask inside her jacket, like a layer between her clothes. She reclassified the smell, recognising it as soot, wondering why on earth she was thinking such thoughts as Tiiu lay on the cabin floor, just a few metres away, and Josef… the masked killer, was, perhaps, even closer.

Against all better judgement, Petra lowered her pistol.

"I'd like to see to my friend," she said, in Danish. "If that's okay, Josef?"

"Your friend is alive."

The voice echoed out of a room towards the back of the cabin, close to the stairs leading to the first floor.

"Yes, and I'm pleased, but I want to see that for myself."

"You don't believe me?"

"You've tricked me once already tonight, Josef." *Keep using his name.* "I'd like to believe you, but I hope you understand if I'm sceptical."

"You're not the woman from the interview."

"No, I'm not." Petra bit her lip and then took a chance. "I'm like you, Josef."

Petra turned her head at a laugh. She looked up,

thinking it came from the first floor.

"No one wants to be like me."

"But we are. Lots of people are like you, Josef."

"What do you know?"

"I know what it's like to grow up in a children's home. The one in Nuuk. The same one as you." Petra listened for a response, then continued in the silence. "I don't know how my parents died. I don't remember them."

"You're lucky."

"I don't think you mean that, Josef."

"Why do you keep saying my name? Is that what they taught you?"

"Yes," Petra said. "I'm a police officer. A commissioner. At least, for a little while longer."

"You're thinking of stopping?"

"I have to." Petra turned her head slowly, as a thin figure stepped out of the shadows. "I promised I would."

"When?"

"As soon as I've helped you."

"You mean as soon as you've arrested me?"

"I won't lie to you, Josef. They sent me here to arrest you." Petra took a small step closer to Tiiu. "Can I talk to my friend?"

"She's unconscious." Josef stepped further into the room. "I hit her."

"Okay. I'm sorry to hear that." Petra pointed at Tiiu. "May I?"

"You're asking my permission?"

"You're in control, Josef. I'm asking for your permission."

"You have it," he said.

Petra holstered her pistol on her way to Tiiu. She crouched by the constable's side, holding her breath as she removed her mask, and then breathing again as Tiiu opened her eyes. Petra pulled the rag from Tiiu's mouth, pressing her lips into a thin smile as she ran her fingers around the back of Tiiu's head, stopping when she found a sticky patch.

"You're going to be okay," she said. "Just lie still."

"Is your friend all right?"

"Yes, Josef." Petra stood up, putting herself between Josef and Tiiu. "Thank you."

"I told you she was."

"You did, and I'm grateful."

"How grateful?"

Petra stared through the dark as Josef approached, searching for features on his pale, thin face. His hair was bunched in a knot above his head, with a stalk of hair bound in sinew below it. His eyes absorbed what little light there was in the room, drawing the darkness into his body, his soul…

Piitalaat…

"Not now, David."

"Who's David?" Josef asked.

"A voice," Petra said. "In my head."

"You hear voices?"

"Yes. Although, I think it's my voice, keeping someone alive, someone dead."

"Someone you loved?"

"Yes. Very much."

"But you can't let him go."

"No, Josef, I can't."

Petra turned as Josef moved to his left, placing himself between her and the cabin door.

"I understand," he said. "I have things I can't let go."

"I noticed."

"What do you mean?"

Petra bristled at the sudden change of tone in Josef's voice. His words grated like glass.

Careful, Piitalaat.

Petra ignored Maratse and forged on, trusting that she had chosen the right path, and that Natuk was somewhere close by.

"You've been working through your pain."

"Yes."

"But, Josef, you've hurt people in the process."

"What process?"

"The purging of your pain. You've killed people to do it."

"It made me feel better."

"Better or powerful, because…"

"What do you know of power?"

"I know a little. But I could tell you more. I have a friend here. He could tell you a lot more."

"You're talking about the professor."

"Yes."

"I almost forgot about him." Josef sighed. "I forget things."

"That's because you hit your head, Josef. When you were little."

"You know a lot, Commissioner. About me. Maybe about power."

"Is the professor all right?"

"He's in one of the other cabins."

"Alive?" Petra took a small step towards Josef. "Is he alive?"

"Yes." Josef leaned forward, jutting his chin over his chest like a tall bird. "Tell me about power. What do you know about it?"

Petra glimpsed Josef's face in a weak cone of light that drifted across the cabins.

"It's a boat," he said, the last of the light fading from his eyes. "I watched it sail up the fjord." He turned back to Petra. "Power. Tell me about it."

Petra caught another whiff of soot in her nose, suddenly aware of the significance of Josef leaving the mask behind on Kaapi's face. Another drift of light crossed the cabin, slightly stronger than the time before. It revealed more of Josef, his head jutting forwards, and his hands clapped tightly to his sides, with a glint of something – metal, perhaps – extending from his fingers.

"I think," Petra said, swallowing, "that you have decided to give up your power."

"Why do you say that?"

"Because you're not wearing your mask."

"I have lots of masks."

"Yes, but only one with any true power." Petra's lips curled at the thought of Lukka's teeth protruding from the mouth of the mask pressing against her chest, inside her jacket. "You gave it to Kaapi to wear."

"After he was dead," Josef said. "He was the counsellor. He talks so much but never listens. He was the best fit to play the role of the one who raped me."

"And Natuk?"

Josef smiled. "She has another role. The final role." His eyes narrowed in another cone of light from the boat nearing the shore. "Tell me about the mask."

"You should have destroyed it."

"Why?"

"It's powerful, Josef. It's a dangerous thing to leave lying around."

"I'm done with it. I don't need its power anymore."

Josef took a step forward, lifting his head as he raised his hands. Petra saw the tools as they flashed in another sweep of light. She heard the distant rumble of the boat's engines but struggled to estimate how close it was.

Not close enough, she thought as she took another look at the tools in Josef's hands.

"I have the mask," she said, reaching for her jacket zip as Josef stalked towards her.

"I know."

"It means I have your power."

"Yes, that's what it means."

Josef raised one hand, stretching his arm wide out to his right, holding the tool at an angle, at neck height. Petra glanced at the other in his left hand, the one he kept low, aimed at her belly. She took a step back, and another, bumping against Tiiu's body, stumbling backwards as Josef lunged forward.

Tiiu groaned as Petra's weight forced the air out of her lungs. Then again, a second time, as Josef's weight pressed down on both of them.

"You have my power," he hissed as Petra gripped his wrists, squeezing them and pushing his arms apart as he jabbed the end of the tools at her face. "Use it."

Petra stared into Josef's eyes. She pulled her head back and tried to butt him in the face, only to jerk in the air halfway towards his chest.

"Use it," he said, spittle flecking Petra's face. "Use the mask."

"It doesn't work like that," Petra said. Her arms trembled as she tried to resist. Josef scrabbled on the floor, working his knees up and onto her legs, crawling up her body, rising above her so he could strike at her head, aiming his forehead at her nose, striking once, then a second time. Petra felt the blood dribble onto her lips. She turned away as he struck again, closing her eyes, ready for impact, only to feel her arms pulled forward, as Josef slid down her body.

"Let go of him, Petra," Natuk said, as she dragged Josef by the ankles, pulling him towards the door. She let go as Josef twisted, pulling Tiiu's pistol from the waistband of her trousers as he slashed at her legs.

"Natuk!" Petra said. "No!"

Natuk flinched as Josef sliced at her trousers, cutting through the thin weave of the lower leg, drawing blood and a curse as he sliced into her skin.

"Damn it." Natuk stepped to one side. She pointed the gun at Josef's head. When he pulled back his arm to slash again, she shifted her aim and shot him once in each knee. Natuk kicked the tools from Josef's hands as he wailed, then stepped around him, pulling Petra to her feet, and then reaching down to help Tiiu stand. "Take this," she said, pressing the pistol into Tiiu's grasp. "Catch your breath, point it at him. Shoot him if he moves. Okay?"

Tiiu shook, drawing one ragged breath after another into her lungs.

"Good girl," Natuk said. She cupped one hand to Tiiu's chin and then kissed her on the cheek. "Remember, if he gets closer, you shoot him."

"Natuk…"

"No time, Commissioner." Natuk stepped away from Tiiu as the light from the boat curved across the beach, brighter now, revealing the blood in Tiiu's hair, and the determined look on Natuk's face. "It's decision time."

"Wait," Petra said, grabbing Natuk's arm as she started for the door. "The professor?"

"First cabin. Sitting on the sofa. I gave him a glass of water and a pep talk. He's going to be fine." Natuk walked to the nearest window, cursing as she stared out at the approaching boat. "That would be the cavalry. The thing about the new commissioner, is that he doesn't stick to the plan. He looked at the weather and must have launched a couple of hours after we did." Natuk looked at Petra. "I don't think your American boyfriend is going to make it. Which is good news, I must admit." She turned to look at Josef as he writhed on the floor. "That's a pathetic mess, right there."

"You shot him, Natuk."

"Yep, but I could have killed him."

"Why didn't you?"

Natuk shrugged, and said, "He got me out of jail. One good deed and all that." She took another look out of the window. "We have to go."

"We?"

"Listen, Petra. I understand things are moving fast, but you have to accept your new reality. You are retired. It's official. And I am on the run. If you want to know who Constable Maratse is hugging in that video, then you'll come with me now. But it has to be now." Natuk patted the trawler keys in her jacket pocket. "I'm not going back to prison."

"Yes, you are," Tiiu said, raising the pistol in her hands.

Natuk laughed, pointed at Tiiu, and said, "Oh, I *really* like this one, Petra. I mean, Aron was cute. But Tiiu…" Natuk pressed her fingers to her lips. "You are full of surprises."

"Lower your gun, Tiiu," Petra said.

"Ma'am?"

"Not anymore. I'm not your boss. But I would like you to lower your gun. Before you get hurt."

"I don't understand."

Petra turned to Tiiu, reached for her gun, and pressed it gently towards the floor. "Natuk says you're full of surprises. But she is not." Petra looked at Natuk, and said, "Show her."

"Whatever you say." Natuk reached into her pocket and pulled out a handful of bullets. "Two was enough," she said. "But you might want these. I'm going to put them here." Natuk dumped the bullets onto the windowsill, smiled once at Tiiu, and then walked out of the cabin.

"Commissioner?" Tiiu said, as Petra took a step

towards the door. "What are you doing?"

"Honestly?" Petra shook her head. "I don't know."

She took the mask out of her jacket and placed in the windowsill beside the bullets. Petra stared at the mask for a moment, tracing the edges with her fingers, searching for the invisible and dark magic that had touched so many people. Her breath caught in her throat and she pulled herself away, tucking her hands into her jacket pockets as she turned back to Tiiu.

"Look after him, Tiiu. And look after yourself," she said, with a nod towards Josef. "Oh, and *Juullimi Pilluaritsi*. Merry Christmas."

Petra followed Natuk out of the door before Tiiu could say anything to change her mind. She called out for Natuk to stop, picking up the pace when she didn't. Petra avoided the looks of the SRU officers, and the skipper's protests. She climbed onto the dock, just as Natuk started the trawler's engine.

"Get the lines, Petra," Natuk said, as she leaned out of the wheelhouse.

"Where are we going?"

"You know where."

Petra gripped the lines in her hand, lifting them slightly as she waited for Natuk to answer her. "Tell me?"

"Don't be so dramatic," Natuk said. "Get on board. We have to go."

"Natuk…"

"Fine, okay." Natuk dropped down from the wheelhouse and walked to the gunwale. "North Star

Bay. Way north of here."

"And what will I find there?"

"Answers."

"And you?"

"Me?" Natuk shrugged. "Freedom, I hope."

Petra untied the lines and tossed them onto the deck. "Okay," she said, as she took Natuk's hand. "Let's go north."

Natuk left Petra on the deck and climbed back into the wheelhouse. She increased the thrust, pulling the trawler away from the dock, and turning the bow into the waves. Petra watched Danielsen's boat – the police cutter – slide along the first dock closest to the cabins. She saw him climb over the side, and considered waving, but stuffed her hands into her pockets instead.

Piitalaat…

"Yes, David. We can talk now. You can tell me all your secrets."

Petra stood at the gunwale, leaning into the side of the boat, as Natuk increased speed, sailing into the dark polar night.

The End

About the Author

Christoffer Petersen is the author's pen name. He lives in Denmark. Chris started writing stories about Greenland while teaching in Qaanaaq, the largest village in the very north of Greenland – the population peaked at 600 during the two years he lived there. Chris spent a total of seven years in Greenland, teaching in remote communities and at the Police Academy in the capital of Nuuk.

Chris continues to be inspired by the vast icy wilderness of the Arctic and his books have a common setting in the region, with a Scandinavian influence. He has also watched enough Bourne movies to no longer be surprised by the plot, but not enough to get bored.

You can find Chris in Denmark or online here:

www.christoffer-petersen.com

By the same Author

THE GREENLAND CRIME SERIES
featuring Constable David Maratse

SEVEN GRAVES, ONE WINTER #1
BLOOD FLOE #2
WE SHALL BE MONSTERS #3
INSIDE THE BEAR'S CAGE #4
WHALE HEART #5

Novellas from the same series

KATABATIC #1
CONTAINER #2
TUPILAQ #3
THE LAST FLIGHT #4
THE HEART THAT WAS A WILD GARDEN #5
QIVITTOQ #6
THE THUNDER SPIRITS #7
ILULIAQ #8
SCRIMSHAW #9
ASIAQ #10
CAMP CENTURY #11
INUK #12
DARK CHRISTMAS #13
POISON BERRY #14
NORTHERN MAIL #15

SIKU #16
VIRUSI #17
BAIT #18
THE WOMEN'S KNIFE #19
ICE, WIND & FIRE #20

Omnibus editions of the Short Stories

CONSTABLE DAVID MARATSE #1
CONSTABLE DAVID MARATSE #2
CONSTABLE DAVID MARATSE #3
CONSTABLE DAVID MARATSE #4
CONSTABLE DAVID MARATSE #5

THE GREENLAND TRILOGY
featuring Konstabel Fenna Brongaard
THE ICE STAR #1
IN THE SHADOW OF THE MOUNTAIN #2
THE SHAMAN'S HOUSE #3

THE POLARPOL ACTION THRILLERS
NORTHERN LIGHT #1
MOUNTAIN GHOST #2

THE DETECTIVE FREJA HANSEN SERIES
FELL RUNNER Introductory novella
BLACKOUT INGÉNUE Book 1

THE WILD CRIME SERIES
featuring Jon and Emma Østergård
PAINT THE DEVIL #1
LOST IN THE WOODS #2
CHERNOBYL WOLVES #3

MADE IN DENMARK
DANISH DESIGN Story 1

THE WHEELMAN SHORTS
PULP DRIVER Story 1

THE DARK ADVENT SERIES
featuring Commissioner Petra Piitalaat Jensen
THE CALENDAR MAN #1
THE TWELFTH NIGHT #2
INVISIBLE TOUCH #3

UNDERCOVER GREENLAND
NARKOTIKA

THE BOLIVIAN GIRL
THE BOLIVIAN GIRL

GUERRILLA GREENLAND
featuring Constable David Maratse
ARCTIC STATE #1
ARCTIC REBEL #2

GREENLAND MISSING PERSONS
featuring Constable Petra Piitalaat Jensen
THE BOY WITH THE NARWHAL TOOTH #1
THE GIRL WITH THE RAVEN TONGUE #2
THE SHIVER IN THE ARCTIC #3
THE FEVER IN THE WATER #4
THE WINTER TRAP #5

Printed in Great Britain
by Amazon

56054670R00156